Clint put off drawing his weapon . . .

. . . simply because there was no doubt in his mind that he could draw his Colt four times before the other man cleared leather once. For most other men, this would have shown an overly ambitious view of their own ability to deal with the situation.

For Clint Adams, it was simple fact.

The other man's hand had just closed around the grip of his pistol and was pulling it upward. His finger curled around the trigger, but was unable to do much more before all motion in his arm was brought to a halt. Clint had already stepped forward and reached out with his left hand to grab hold of the man's wrist and dig his thumb between the veins running along the underside of his arm.

Keeping his eyes locked on the face of the man right in front of him, Clint tightened his grip until he saw the other man wince in pain . . .

"Not a smart move," Clint said in a quiet, warning tone.

THE GUNSMITH

268

BIG-SKY BANDITS

J. R. ROBERTS

JOVE BOOKS, NEW YORK

BIG-SKY BANDITS

A Jove Book / published by arrangement with
the author

PRINTING HISTORY
Jove edition / April 2004

ISBN: 0-515-13717-0

A JOVE BOOK®
Jove Books are published by The Berkley Publishing Group,
a division of Penguin Group (USA) Inc.,
375 Hudson Street, New York, New York 10014.
JOVE and the "J" design
are trademarks belonging to Penguin Group (USA) Inc.

PRINTED IN THE UNITED STATES OF AMERICA

10 9 8 7 6 5 4 3 2 1

ONE

Most of the time, Clint listened to his gut.

That first instinct was usually the right one, and more often than not, it knew the best way to go. For a man to have walked through as much fire as Clint Adams and still be able to walk at all, he had to know when to listen.

Clint was a gambling man, so he knew better than most when to listen to his gut above everything else. Even with all of this in mind, however, Clint knew his instincts weren't always the right ones.

Everyone made mistakes, no matter where they got their advice.

Just under a week ago, Clint's gut had told him to ride southeast. It didn't seem like a momentous decision at the time, especially since he'd already been headed in that direction anyway. Since Clint was a man who enjoyed his freedom and rode wherever he felt the wind pull him, he didn't think twice about his choice of direction when he'd first pointed the nose of his Darley Arabian stallion southeast and flicked the reins. Eclipse was always up for a good run and didn't seem to mind where he was headed any more than the man on his back.

1

Clint's travels had most recently taken him south through California and past the city of Fresno. In fact, he even knew several towns along the way he could visit should he need to stop for a night to rest or get some more supplies. The scenery was beautiful. Summer was coming into full bloom, and all seemed right with the world.

All was right, that is, until he caught his first glimpse of the desert.

The desert wasn't the kind of thing that snuck up on a man. The travelers who stumbled into it usually didn't stumble out again. Nature has a way of weeding out the folks who are too stupid to deserve a spot beneath another sunset. Those folks can usually be found in a saloon shooting their mouths off to anyone who will listen.

Those are also the types who wind up dead in those same saloons or crying to the sheriff when a sharper mind comes by to give them something to cry about. When it came to traveling on the open trail, those were the ones whose stories ended up with phrases like, "and they were never seen again."

In the desert, those people usually ended up as lonely, sunbaked skeletons lying half-buried in the sand. The only good thing they accomplished was providing a free set of boots and a hat to the next poor soul who happened along.

Those are the cold, hard facts. You can think of them what you will, but nature doesn't give a damn what you think.

Shaking his head, Clint gazed at the land stretched out before him and focused on the desert he was approaching. He'd ridden through this area before. He sure as hell knew the desert was there. He just didn't know that a trip through the sand was high on his priorities at that point in time.

Then again, thinking about stupid men and the harsh way nature dealt with them, Clint knew there was a better reason for him to have come that way apart from dumb luck.

Whenever he rode to cover distance, he always kept his mind full of places to stop along the way. That was just good sense and this time had been no different. Tugging back on Eclipse's reins, he brought the stallion to a stop and stretched his back.

After straightening some of the kinks from his neck, Clint turned his attention to the trail ahead and focused on what had brought him to the brink of the unforgiving desert right at the start of the hot season. The Darley Arabian shifted beneath him, grateful for the pause yet also a bit eager to continue. In that way, the horse was a lot like its rider.

It was the latter half of the day and the sun was still high in the sky. Although not beating down directly on top of his head, it gave off enough heat that it seemed to be creeping beneath his skin. When he glanced up, Clint saw waves of heat pulsing out from its sun's fiery center, making it appear close enough to touch.

The ground beneath Eclipse's hooves was a mixture of packed soil and clay. Sprouts of thick grass pushed upward in green clumps as if defying the source of light overhead. With only a few wisps of clouds in the sky, there was enough light to illuminate the earth for miles in every direction. Clint didn't even need to use his spyglass to see where the rest of his day's journey would take him.

On the horizon, sitting there like an answer he should have known all along, was a few dark shapes that were too blocky and symmetrical to be natural. Smoke swirled up from a few of the shapes, confirming the fact that those were indeed buildings he'd spotted.

All Clint had to do was look at those buildings for the name of the town to spring into his mind.

Cielo Grande.

That was Spanish for "big sky" and was one hell of an understatement for the way miles of blue stretched out over all of God's creation.

Clint wasn't a stupid man. He hadn't just wandered too close to the desert without knowing any better. He'd even had the name of that town in the back of his mind as one of those places to stop for supplies or a night in a bed rather than sleeping on the ground. He'd figured he might stay there since he would probably reach the town at the end of a punishing ride.

But even with all that considering, he hadn't truly thought anything else about Cielo Grande apart from the name. It wasn't until he'd stopped and mulled it over that he saw the town as more than a stop along the way. There was more to the town than that.

A whole lot more.

When he started reminding himself about the last time he'd been to Cielo Grande, Clint quickly remembered why he'd done his best to try and forget the place.

TWO

It had been just a little over three years since Clint had last been on his way into Cielo Grande. In many respects, that time wasn't too much different from the second one. Both times, Clint's mind had been filled with everything from the scenery to the desert ahead. And each time, he'd been on his way to somewhere else.

Nobody in their right mind came to Cielo Grande as their first choice. The place was a decent size, but each building looked as though it had been burned or knocked down at least once and cobbled back together again . . . badly.

Every structure leaned slightly one way or another and stayed upright mainly because the wind wasn't prone to kicking up more than a few gouts of dust. That wind whistled through the cracks in the poorly maintained buildings, giving the breeze a strange chorus of whistles that would make any self-respecting carpenter wince.

Even the streets were crooked thanks to the uneven tilt of every store and home. The water troughs leaked and the glass in most of the windows was either broken or so dirty that it might as well have been painted over.

But despite all its faults, Cielo Grande was the type of place that felt like its half-assed buildings would be standing for a good, long time. After all, if they hadn't fallen over already, odds were good that they'd be there longer than most of the residents. There was a good number of people living there and they seemed like decent enough folks.

At least, this had been Clint's impression when he'd ridden into town that first time three years ago. . . .

He'd been heading south on his way to Texas and was doing his best to skirt the desert rather than ride through the harsh dunes. He was in no hurry, so there was no good reason for him to take any unnecessary risks.

When Clint arrived in Cielo Grande those three years ago, his first impulse had been to look up and take a glance at the town's namesake. Being on the edge of a barren expanse of desert, the town felt like an oasis. The winds even seemed to lose their strength before rattling anything in town more than a little.

The sky was full of clouds and seemed to stretch out over him like an ocean. It seemed so wide and massive, that Clint felt a touch of dizziness when he'd tried looking up at it for more than a few seconds. He pulled in a deep breath to clear his head and rode to the first livery he could find, which was a large barn that seemed older than the dirt on its floor.

Clint found it somewhat amusing that his horse seemed to get finicky as soon as he saw that he was headed for the rickety building. For a few moments he even felt bad about leaving his animal there, but then he saw that the livery was probably older than he was and wasn't going anywhere anytime soon.

Like most of the other folks he'd seen on his way in,

the young man who worked at the stable seemed nice enough even though he was just as gritty as the building where he worked. He accepted Clint's money with a crooked smile and just enough conversation to pass the time until the animal was put into a stall. From there, Clint was on his own.

While walking through another section of town, Clint quickly saw what had made the horse feel more than a little uneasy. There was a tension in the air that didn't come from any passing storm. It was the kind of underlying tension that one might feel if they were a little too far down inside a mine where the support timbers were beginning to rot and shift.

Although the locals appeared to be going about their daily routines, the casual looks on their faces were obviously forced. It was one of those things that Clint might have missed before simply because he hadn't been paying close attention. Now that he was looking in the right places, however, his gambling instincts kicked in and told him what was going on.

If he'd seen those people sitting across a card table from him, Clint would have taken everything he heard from their mouths with a grain of salt. The somewhat trembling smiles screamed of a bluff. The uneasy, shifting eyes all but told him straightaway that the locals had been dealt a losing hand and were trying their best to get out with their skins intact.

Now that he'd spotted the unusual behavior, Clint did his best to try and pin down its source. As he walked by every one of the locals, he tipped his hat and engaged them in conversation, even if only for a word or two.

"Hello there," he said to an elderly couple walking arm-in-arm.

Both the gray-haired man and woman did their best to

put on a warm smile and return the sentiment. Their words, however, were a little forced and their pace picked up considerably until they'd walked past Clint completely.

The next people Clint encountered were a group of the men who appeared to be a few years younger than he was. Each of them was dressed in the worn leathers of a cowboy and had the muscular build that usually put more confidence in a fellow's stride.

Clint tipped his hat and took on an easy swagger as he said, "Howdy," in a tone that seemed to fit the three men just fine.

They might have reacted in a friendly way at first, but in the space of a heartbeat, they were looking just as nervous as those two old-timers who were still hustling in the other direction. All three of the young men tensed visibly. They might have just been no good at bluffing, but Clint got the feeling it was something else.

Since the three men didn't move quite as fast as the elderly couple, Clint got a chance to study them more closely. In that time, he saw a bitter look under the surface of all three of those faces. They had the look about them of men trying to swallow some bitter medicine.

And it seemed as though that bitter medicine was damn near turning their stomachs. Still, they plastered on tense smiles and walked a little faster until Clint was out of their sight.

He passed plenty of others, but Clint didn't have to study them half as hard. The first handful of locals had told him enough just by the way they reacted. Not only were they tense and nervous about something, but they were hiding something as well.

Not only were they hiding something, but they were watching Clint very carefully also.

But the thing that really made Clint feel a little nervous

was the fact that none of the locals was wearing guns. Not a single one of them. And when they spotted the modified Colt at Clint's side, they each looked back at him with the same face as a dog that fully expects to get a whipping.

And when that whipping didn't come right away, they looked at him for a brief moment as though they might have expected something from him. It wasn't in the eyes of every single person he met, but Clint did pick this up in enough of them to catch his attention.

Before he could think too much about it, he spotted a group of three men turning a nearby corner and stopping to take a look up and down the street. They turned their heads slowly, taking in their surroundings like proud rulers out for a stroll in their kingdom. These men were different from the rest.

First of all, they had nothing but smug confidence in their demeanor. Second, they were all wearing gun belts. Clint had no doubt in his mind that one had a great deal to do with the other. And when they spotted Clint, that confidence flared up into outright cockiness.

The flicker of emotion that Clint had spotted in the townspeople was still there. In fact, it grew when they saw that Clint was obviously not with the three armed men. There was still fear written across the townspeople's faces, but when they caught Clint's eyes, they displayed something else entirely.

Hope.

THREE

The people who'd been walking down the street parted like the Red Sea for the three armed men. When the three men threw an occasional look at them, the locals averted their eyes and did their best to try and blend in with their surroundings.

Clint knew it was too late to avoid the trio and he wasn't about to run from them. As much as he liked to stay away from snap judgments, he couldn't help but dislike the three armed men. There was just something about them that set the hairs on the back of his neck on end. They strutted like bullies and the smug grins on their faces were just begging to be knocked off.

It might have been the heat or the long ride, but Clint was fairly certain neither of those things was to blame for his bad mood more than the trio strutting right for him. Clint watched the three men very closely and couldn't help but notice something about all of them that was a definite tip-off regarding their true characters.

Each of them flinched slightly when they saw the gun strapped around Clint's waist. Not only that, their hands dropped to rest upon the grips of their own weapons as

if just feeling the pistols still in place gave them the other
half of their confidence.

There was plenty of time to study the trio since they
all made a show of the fact that they were in no hurry to
get where they were going. During the dramatic, arrogant
show, Clint sized up the men based on what he could see.
He didn't even need half of the time he was given to
complete the task.

Even the guns they wore were the kind favored by
blowhards. Big, older model Colts, which were intimidating in their size and caliber. They were loud, powerful
weapons but also heavy and outdated. Clint figured he'd
get even money if he bet that those guns weren't fired at
much more than empty bottles or jackrabbits.

Just to be on the safe side, Clint spent the rest of the
time given to him to make himself appear a little cowed.
Such a simple thing would certainly buy him plenty of
breathing room from arrogant pricks like those three.

Finally the trio came to a stop less than two paces away
from Clint. The man in the middle was wiry and shifty-
eyed with a mess of tangled black hair jutting out from
beneath his hat. He wore a face full of whiskers and
reeked as if he hadn't bathed in months.

Standing on either side of him were two bigger men,
taller but not as muscular as the one in the middle. Most
of their size came from thick barrel-chests and solid bel-
lies, which hung slightly over their belts. One wore his
hair like a ten-year-old kid, neatly combed and parted as
if done by his mother. The other bigger man's hair was
nothing but short, sweaty stubble. This one wore a goatee
flecked with bits of dirt.

Smirking as if he knew damn well Clint was too scared
to talk, the man in the middle waited a few seconds before
saying, "You're new in town. Just passing through?"

"That was the idea," Clint replied. "You know any good hotels around here?"

"Sure do," the doughy one with the parted hair said. "Place called Emma's Palace. It's two or three towns over."

The other two in the little group found that amusing enough and glanced at each other to show that they were laughing. Although they were standing a good distance away to watch, the locals who'd been in the area were dead quiet.

Clint smiled at them, but didn't laugh with them. He doubted either of the three would notice the difference.

They didn't.

"I think I'd prefer something a little closer," Clint said once the laughter had died down a bit. "That is, if it's all the same to you."

When he added that last part, Clint knew full well that he was giving one of the men the opening they'd been waiting for. But rather than just simply goading the armed men, Clint thought of himself more as a fisherman. The hook was baited, so now it was time to see what he might catch.

The muscular guy in the middle was only too eager to bite. In fact, he nearly snapped his head forward as though he truly was going to live up to the comparison. "Well it's not all the same to me," he said, adding what was intended to be a threatening snarl to his voice. "What's all the same to me is you turning your ass around and getting out of this town. Why don't you take the advice my friend already gave you? It sure would be a whole lot healthier."

Clint raised his eyebrows innocently just to stir things up a little more. "Healthier? Is there some kind of flu going around? Oh, I know. Maybe there's something in the water here. Is that why you and your friends haven't bathed for at least . . . what? . . . a month or two?"

All three armed men recoiled slightly as though they thought Clint were insane. All around them, the locals went from being frightened to trying their best to keep from laughing. Despite all the changes that washed through the people, not a single sound was made.

The only things that could be heard were wheels crunching over dry dirt and horses calling out as reins were snapped. Other conversations went on, but none in the immediate area.

For everyone standing on that street, the world might just as well stopped turning. All eyes were jumping between Clint and the three armed men. All mouths were hanging at least slightly open and all ears were open, anxiously awaiting the response that was sure to come.

Even though he could feel the seconds dragging by just like everyone else, Clint acted as though he'd said nothing out of the ordinary. He just kept dangling that hook in front of the three to see what would happen. Just as he'd figured, neither of the other two were about to do so much as nibble at the bait until they got word from the one in the middle.

The armed man standing between the other two cocked his head to one side, looked around to see that he was being watched closely by everyone else and made a quick grab for his gun.

FOUR

Clint had been ready for one of those gunmen to make their move from the moment he saw them strutting toward him. Each of them had trouble written all over their faces, and all he wanted to do was see which of them would be more trouble than the other two. That would tell Clint which of the three was the leader and how big of a threat these men truly were.

After all, just because a man wears a gun and struts around with it doesn't mean he's got the sand to pull it on anyone. Well now that Clint had the answers to his questions, he had to deal with the consequences.

The instant he saw one of the men going for his gun, Clint put himself into the frame of mind that saw him through most fights. He focused intently on his target and his mind raced three steps ahead of the game.

Clint put off drawing his own weapon simply because he had no doubt in his mind that he could draw his Colt four times before the other man cleared leather once. For most other men, this would have shown an overly ambitious view of their own ability to deal with the situation.

For Clint Adams, however, this was simple fact.

The other man's hand had just closed around the grip of his pistol and was pulling it upward. His finger curled around the trigger, but was unable to do much more before all motion in his arm was brought to a halt. Clint had already stepped forward and reached with his left hand out to grab hold of his wrist and dig his thumb between the veins running along the underside of his arm.

Keeping his eyes locked on the face of the man right in front of him, Clint tightened his grip until he saw the other man wince in pain. From there, he twisted his hand and wrenched outward until the guy wasn't even able to hold on to his pistol any longer. Clint kept on twisting, forcing the other man's hand a good foot and a half from his holster.

"Not a smart move," Clint said in a quiet, warning tone. "What about your friends? Are they stupid enough to make the same mistake?"

Glancing at both of the men flanking the one in the middle, Clint saw that they'd started to go for their weapons, but stopped in mid-draw. One had a good grip around the gun's handle, but hadn't even started to lift it out. The one with the stubble-covered scalp was a little further along, but didn't pull his gun out the rest of the way.

"What should we do, Dutch?" the big man with the neatly parted hair asked.

Clint nodded and put on a smile that he knew would stoke the fires burning inside all three men. "Dutch, is it? Well, if I were you, Dutch, I'd cut my losses and keep on walking to wherever you were headed before meeting me."

The man with the stubble curled his lips in a semblance of a snarl. The grimace would have been much more intimidating if he wasn't so indecisive about whether or not he should even move. "We can take him, Dutch. Just say the word and this asshole is—"

"Shut the hell up, Jim," Dutch barked. "You too, Andy. Or are the both of you blind as well as stupid?"

Jim and Andy were obviously confused by that. To clarify himself even further, Dutch nodded downward to draw the other two's eyes toward Clint. It was only then that the two bigger men saw that Clint's right hand was closed around his modified Colt.

Unlike any of the other three, Clint's gun hand wasn't frozen. It was steady as a rock and it didn't take much of a thinker to realize that if he'd moved so quickly with his left hand, his gun hand was undoubtedly twice as fast.

Dutch kept his eyes glued to Clint's face while the other two darted their glances back and forth between Clint, Dutch and their remaining partner. The stunned expressions on the two bigger men's faces was fading away and their courage was coming back to them in little drips.

Seeing that, Clint knew he had to catch their attention once more. Without waiting another second, he used his left hand to toss aside Dutch's gun hand. Before any of the three could react, Clint had already plucked the gun from Dutch's holster, drawn his own Colt and taken a step back.

Once again, all three of the other men were caught frozen in mid-motion. Clint held the guns at hip level, aiming at a point on either side of Dutch and in between all three. Snapping back the hammers of both pistols made a metallic click that spoke louder than any voice.

"All right then," Clint said. "Let's try this one more time. Rather than ask how stupid you fellas are, I'll just presume the worst and tell you what I want you to hear." Smiling a little wider, he added, "And I'll be sure to speak slowly and use short words.

"If any of those guns of yours moves anywhere but down into their holsters, I'll shoot all three of you."

The trio bristled at that, but complied. Dutch kept his hands up and out slightly while the other two eased their guns back into their resting places at their sides.

"Now drop those gun belts and step back," Clint ordered.

If looks could kill, Clint as well as everyone else on that street would have been in the ground. The three men's eyes gave off pure, intense hatred as they unbuckled their gun belts and let them fall. From there, they stepped back and fixed Clint with an even more intense stare.

Clint nodded and relaxed a bit, but kept his guns trained on the three men. "I've got things to do, so I want someone here to fetch the law and collect these guns. Is that simple enough for you?"

Clint waited until he got nods from the three men lined up in front of him.

"Good. Now, do I even have to tell you that this is the only warning you get?" Clint asked. His voice lost every bit of its sarcasm and the smile on his face melted away when he added, "Because if I have to put up with this kind of bullshit from the likes of you while I'm here, I won't be half as understanding as I was this time."

Clint didn't have to say much more than that to get his point across. He stared straight into each of the three men's eyes until each one of them looked away. It was the oldest test of mettle known to man and Clint won on all three counts.

Of course, that didn't mean that Clint was about to turn his back on them either. Not wanting to waste any more time with them, Clint stepped back and lowered his guns as he went.

"Go on, now," he said to the trio. "Get moving."

The tone in Clint's voice left no room for discussion. The words were not requests and they were not suggestions. They were commands, pure and simple. Since he was the one holding a pistol in each fist, Clint stood and watched as the other three carried out his command to the letter.

Dutch turned around first and then the other two followed suit. Grumbling just enough to show their contempt for the situation, but being quiet enough to keep from being understood fully, the men walked back down the street the same way they'd come. Their guns and holsters stayed behind, along with no small amount of their pride.

That heavy, sustained silence fell upon the street once more. It stayed there the entire time Dutch, Andy and Jim dragged themselves out of Clint's sight and turned the corner. Even after they'd gone, the trio's presence could still be seen reflected in the frightened stares of all the astonished locals.

Every eye in the vicinity turned to look at Clint. Every jaw was hanging open at least a little in blatant shock.

Once it was certain that the three were gone for the moment and not about to come running back, those locals who'd been watching the scene took a deep breath. When they let it out, they did so by raising their fists in the air and letting out a cheer that rolled down the street like thunder.

FIVE

After all the things he'd done in his life, no matter how many lives he'd saved or bad men he'd faced down, it was truly rare that Clint felt like a hero. There was always something else that needed doing and plenty of good deeds came along at the worst times anyhow. Walking away from a gunfight was reward enough and his soul paid the price for every man he'd been forced to kill.

For all of those reasons, Clint rarely got to enjoy the fruits of his labor. On the contrary, it was usually everyone around him who enjoyed the end result of all his hard work. But that wasn't the case on that street in Cielo Grande those years ago.

Seeing the looks on those faces and all those eager smiles, Clint had felt larger than life. Somewhere deep down inside, he actually felt as though he'd lived up to what was written about him in all those terrible yellowback novels that were supposedly about his life.

Even as he sat high in Eclipse's saddle outside the town three years later while thinking back on it, Clint felt a rush of blood flow through his face. That flush of pride was just as strong now as it had been back then. The smile on his face wasn't quite as bright as it had been that day, but it still reflected how the locals had made him feel.

For a moment, Clint had to close his eyes in order to throw himself back fully into that moment. When he did that, he could actually hear the raised voices that had come after those three men had been forced to turn and walk away from a fight.

Clint could actually feel the anxious hands slapping him on the back or grasping his own for a quick shake as he walked by. The sun had felt much the same beating down on the back of his neck then as it did now, making it that much easier to relive the moment. . . .

He'd been so taken aback by the reception he'd gotten that Clint nearly tripped over the gun belts which were still lying in the street. While just meaning to move on and get back to his business, Clint was nearly knocked over by the rush of people who wanted to give him their thanks in a more up-close manner.

The first dozen thank-you's had been clear enough, but very quickly they degenerated into a wash of sound. Voices blended together to form something close to waves beating against rocks as too many people tried to say too many things in too short a time.

Clint did his best to shake as many hands as he could and acknowledge as many smiles as humanly possible before eventually breaking off and shouldering his way through the crowd. As soon as he was no longer in the middle of them all, Clint heard the crowd's cheers and congratulations ease off a bit. There were a few more hands reaching out to pat him on the back before the group disbanded.

Clint felt like he was breaking the surface of the water after being held under for too long. His heart was beating at a quicker pace, and he could feel his cheeks were flushed. Most of that came from being suddenly surrounded by so many people. Although there couldn't have been more than a dozen or two, they were so close that it felt like ten times that number.

Just to be certain, Clint stopped once he got onto the boardwalk and took a look over his shoulder. Some of the locals who were still looking at him gave a quick wave, but for the most part it seemed as though people had gotten back to their business.

When Clint turned around again, he nearly jumped out of his skin. Standing only a foot or so from him was a figure who seemed to have dropped from the sky. Clint had heard the approach of footsteps, but thought they were still a little ways off. Apparently, the person doing the stepping was just a bit lighter than he'd guessed.

"Jesus," Clint said when he damn near walked into a woman, who hadn't been standing there the last time he'd checked.

She was tall for a woman, standing almost at Clint's height. Her hair was mostly dark brown, but had lighter, almost golden, streaks running through it, which had come from being kissed by the sun's rays. She smiled at Clint with lips that were the perfect contrast; the upper was close to bow-shaped, while the lower was plump and soft.

Although her nose was a little wide, it fit perfectly with the rest of her face. Even her eyes, which were the same color as most of her hair, were just a little wider than normal with luxurious lashes to match. Although most of her body was covered by a tan-and-white dress, Clint could see plenty of her smooth skin which was the color of lightly creamed coffee.

"Sorry," she said while taking half a step back. "I didn't mean to startle you."

Clint shook his head and gave her a wide smile. "I'm just a little on edge, is all. Good thing I turned around before bumping into you."

With a warmer, more seductive smile of her own, she replied, "That wouldn't have been so bad."

"No. Actually it wouldn't. My name's Clint."

"Sofia," she said while holding out one hand palm-down.

Clint took the opportunity he'd been given and wrapped his hand gently around hers. The woman's skin was warm and soft to the touch, surpassing even Clint's own expectations. Lifting her hand to his lips, he kissed her once and let her go.

Bowing his head a bit for the formal greeting allowed Clint a closer look at her large, rounded breasts. Even though the dress wasn't particularly revealing, the top section was held together by thin, leather laces which let him get a nice glance at her truly impressive cleavage.

Clint took all this in without allowing his eyes to linger for a disrespectful amount of time. "I wouldn't want to keep you from anything, Sofia."

"You're not. Actually, I wanted to come here and talk to you." Seeming a little embarrassed, she lowered her eyes and said, "I saw what you did just now. You're very brave."

"Eh, those three were all bluster."

"But still, I'd like to thank you."

"No need for that."

"Please Clint," Sofia said while reaching out to take him by the hand. "I insist."

SIX

When she took him by the hand and led him down the boardwalk, Clint's mind filled with various scenarios. All of those involved the two of them being in more secluded surroundings getting to know each other a whole lot better.

Where they'd wound up was a small, family-owned restaurant, sharing a table that was just big enough to hold the soup and sandwiches she'd ordered. It was a bit early for lunch, but the day had been full enough for Clint to work up an appetite. Also, it gave him something to do while he tried to put his more hopeful thoughts out of his head.

"How's this?" Sofia asked. "I know it's not too fancy, but I know the owners."

Clint smiled and wiped his mouth before answering. "It's great. You really didn't have to do anything like this."

"I felt like if nobody else was gonna do more than slap you on the back, then I would be the one to thank you for what you did. You don't know how long we've all

been waiting for someone to put Dutch and his boys in
their place like that."

"So I take it he does more than shoot his mouth off?"

"Yes," Sofia answered. "A lot more sometimes. He's
killed half a dozen men since he got here. That bastard's
got folks so scared that they don't even wear guns no
more just so they don't get on Dutch's bad side."

Hearing that brought back the thoughts Clint had been
forming earlier when he'd noticed just how many people
walked around unarmed. It wasn't unusual for locals to
leave their guns at home while they were out and about.
What had struck Clint as odd was the fact that he'd seen
not even a single weapon since he'd entered town. Now,
he knew why.

"What about the law?" Clint asked.

"Oh, Sheriff Curtis told Dutch to get the hell out of
this town and not come back."

"Well, there you go. He sounds like a stand-up man."

"He was. He stood up right until the moment that a
few of Dutch's boys shot him in the back. Since then, we
haven't exactly had a rush of men wanting to fill that job."

Where Clint had been thinking of the three men he'd
met as pushy blowhards, he now started to see them in a
different light. Bullying locals was one thing. Killing them
and gunning down a lawman were other things entirely.

Sofia's face had darkened as though a cloud had passed
in front of her light. She shook it off and shrugged, putting
on a weary smile. "But even the sheriff didn't get half as
close as you did out there." Her smile became brighter
when she added, "I even saw old man Johnson running
off with Dutch's guns. Can you beat it?"

Before Clint could answer, the front door to the restaurant flew open and a boy no more than nine years old
came running through. His feet slammed against the floor-

boards and his breath raced in and out of his heaving chest. "Marc Abels down at the livery just saw Dutch and the rest of them collect their horses and leave!"

The old man who'd taken Clint and Sofia's order seemed to regain ten years of his youth as he bolted from the back of the room to the front. He swept up the little kid off his feet and spoke excitedly directly into his face. "What did you say?"

Although a little surprised at the old man's speed, the kid was too excited to object to being picked up like a rag doll. "Dutch and the rest just collected their horses and rode out of town!"

"All of them?"

"Yes, sir. Mister Abels handed over the reins himself. He saw Dutch take all his boys and ride away. He said they had full saddlebags and everything like they wasn't even plannin' on coming back!"

The old man turned around and started to run back to his wife, who was waiting at the kitchen door. Before he took more than a step, he set the kid down and then high-tailed it to the gray-haired woman.

"Oh my lord," Sofia said in an excited whisper.

Clint leaned back in his chair and took a look out the window. "I know," he said while glancing up and down the street outside. "I'm just glad he'd already brought us our soup."

"You're really sure about this?" Sofia asked the kid, who'd been just about to dash off to his next stop in spreading the news.

The kid glanced over his shoulder and nodded once. "Yes, ma'am. My pa told me it were true. He talked to Miss Anderson and she said Dutch was gone for good and my pa don't ever lie."

With that bit of finality, the kid turned and flew

through the door as if his britches were on fire. Sofia smiled partly because of that and partly because of what the kid had said.

"Did you hear that?" she asked, wheeling around to embrace Clint. "You did it. You truly did it!"

"Well, I'm not sure if—" But Clint couldn't get the rest of his sentence out before Sofia's lips were pressed against his own. Her kiss was long and full of fire, made even hotter by the flick of her tongue against his skin.

"Trust me," she said softly once she pulled away just a little. "Dutch is mean, but full of wind. Plenty of us have been saying that all it would take is someone standing up to him once to drive him off. You came and did just that and he left, just like we said."

"He might come back, you know," Clint warned.

"Let him. I'd say after seeing Dutch run off once, the men around here will start acting like men again. They'll handle him. But in the meantime . . ." She let her words trail off and pressed her body against Clint's.

Sofia wrapped her arms around him and ran the tips of her fingers along Clint's back. From there, she traced her hands upward, over his neck and then raked them through his hair. All the while, she took Clint's breath away with a kiss that just kept coming at him.

Her lips moved over his. Her breath worked quickly in and out of her mouth, mingling with his until they shared the same air. Every so often, she would nibble gently on his lower lip before licking the spot where her teeth had just been.

When the kiss was finally over, Clint could barely pull any air into his lungs. His eyes focused on her and his body reacted instantly to the way her full breasts were pressed against him and the brush of her rounded hips against his own.

"I was going to save that for later," she whispered into his ear. "But I just couldn't wait."

"Fine by me. I'll take a little early taste of dessert any-time."

Taking hold of his hand, Sofia walked backward to-ward the door, dragging Clint along with her. "You just wait until I get you alone," she said. "That's when you'll get more dessert than you can handle."

Clint was in no mood to argue.

SEVEN

Cielo Grande was small enough of a town that the entire place was brimming with excitement as Clint and Sofia walked down the streets. If he hadn't known any better, Clint might have thought that someone had announced the end of a war or the coming of some surprise celebration judging by all the smiling faces and excited cheering.

The locals were chattering excitedly among themselves and the little boy was still running from one door to another, stirring things up into an absolute frenzy. At least that was the way it seemed from where Clint was standing.

Looking back, things might not have been quite as riled up as all that. Then again, it might have also been that he was pretty riled up on his own thanks to the constant attention he got from Sofia as she led him to her house down the street. One thing he was sure of was that there was excitement coursing through Cielo Grande that afternoon, and plenty of it.

Although most of the louder commotion was gone by the time Clint stepped up to Sofia's door, he could still see more folks on the street than there had been before.

They were still talking back and forth in a rush, but were also getting back to their own business.

Their steps may have been lighter and their smiles wider, but there was still things that needed to be done. There were still lives that needed to be led.

Sofia, on the other hand, seemed completely absorbed in Clint's eyes. The only time she looked away from him was to make sure she was headed in the right direction. And once she got onto the familiar ground of her own front steps, there was no need for her to stop watching him even that long.

Holding both of Clint's hands, she led him into a narrow door that opened directly onto the boardwalk. Her home was a narrow house connected to a general store on one side and a similar home on the other. Although the room was noticeably narrow, it ran all the way along the length of the neighboring store. At the back of the room was a set of stairs leading to the upper floor.

Judging by the looks of the front parlor, Sofia hadn't been expecting guests. There were various knickknacks lying around and several pieces of clothing scattered over the backs of chairs and draped over a worn-out sofa. Moving between the clutter was like a strange sort of dance as Sofia led the way while stepping backward toward the steps.

Her and Clint's feet maneuvered around obstacles of all sizes until they got to the back of the room. Even though Clint wasn't watching much of anything else besides Sofia's face, he could tell they were in a kitchen by the sweet smell of bread that hung in the air.

"Come on, Clint," she said in a voice that sounded more like a playful growl. "Time for dessert."

She'd stepped backward up the first four steps, pulling Clint along while shifting her hips to tempt him even fur-

ther. Her eyes widened when Clint's hands snapped out
of her grasp and leapt forward until they closed around
her waist.

Tightening his grip until she stopped trying to wriggle
away, Clint pulled her close while climbing up to stand
on the step directly beneath hers. When she started to fall
forward, he braced himself against the wall with his hip
and the bottom step with his back leg. That was more
than enough to steady himself so he could catch her.

"Actually," he said, lowering her just a little more until
he was practically dipping her the way a dancer would on
a ballroom floor, "I was thinking about having my dessert
now. That is, if that's all right with you."

The moment that last word was spoken, Clint leaned
down to give her a kiss that would steal her breath away
in much the same way that she'd stolen his in that restaurant not too long ago.

It worked.

Her arms tightened around him and she began moaning
softly into his mouth. From there, Clint kept leaning her
back until she was resting on the stairs. He shifted his
weight so that he was on top of her, straddling her with
one knee resting on a stair on either side of her.

Sofia looked around as though she was just realizing
where she was, and a naughty smile crept onto her face.
"My bedroom is right at the top of the stairs," she said.

Clint shook his head. "I don't care about that. I don't
want to wait until we get to the top of the stairs." As he
spoke, his hands were roaming down her leg until he
could hook his fingertips around the bottom hem of her
skirt. He slowly moved his hand upward, peeling up the
fabric of her dress as he went.

Sofia leaned her head back as a chill ran through her
body. The touch of Clint's fingers upon her skin was

something she'd been wanting to feel, and yet she was still surprised when it came. Perhaps it was where they were or maybe she was still a little shocked to have him there at all. Either way, it felt good, and she wasn't about to do a thing to stop him.

Although the stairs were more than a little awkward, the adjustments they had to make were well worth the effort. Clint balanced himself upon the edge of another step while Sofia shifted until she found a somewhat steady place to lie.

It seemed as though they found the perfect spot at the same time. Not only did they keep from falling, but their bodies came together in a way that felt like they were made to be together. Clint's erect penis pressed against his clothing and rubbed into the warm spot between Sofia's legs. That simple touch, even through the material they wore, was enough to send them both to new heights of desire.

Sofia pulled at the strings holding the top of her blouse together while Clint straightened up and tore off his shirt. For a few moments, their hands worked feverishly to get their clothes off. Clint fought with his jeans while Sofia wriggled out of her dress until it was bunched around her waist and one leg was free.

It wasn't perfection, but it was close enough. With bits of clothing still hanging off an arm or leg, they turned their attention back to each other and picked up right where they left off. Clint changed his mind the moment his cock drove deep into her warm pussy.

It was perfection.

EIGHT

Sofia reached out with both arms to grab on to anything so she could steady herself while Clint pumped into her. One hand pressed against a wall while the other wrapped around a wooden pole supporting the banister. Her knuckles went white as she felt him drive all the way inside of her, burying every inch of his rigid cock between her legs.

With one hand placed on the stair next to Sofia's head, Clint used his free hand to take hold of her plump backside and lift her up for every thrust. Her skirts were still tangled around her legs just as Clint's own clothes were still hanging on to him in one way or another. That only made the encounter wilder and more intense.

Since he didn't have either hand free, Clint looked down at Sofia's body, letting his eyes roam over her skin the way he wished his fingers could. Her large breasts rocked in time to the rhythm of their bodies. Every time he pushed into her, he could see the round, dark nipples becoming more erect.

Even the parts of her body that were normally covered from the sun, Sofia's skin was smooth and dark. The color reminded Clint of light caramel. Clint couldn't help but notice that she had the spice of a Mexican, but also the exotic flavor of a Spaniard. Soon, she began to moan in Spanish while gripping the banister support even tighter.

"Dios, mio," she groaned from between clenched teeth. "Oh, *dios, mio!"*

They were quickly becoming accustomed to their surroundings and their bodies were finding more and better ways to maintain balance. Clint closed one hand over Sofia's, which was in turn wrapped around the wooden pole. Moving his foot up to a higher step, he pumped his hips back and forth in a way that caused Sofia's eyes to snap open and roll upward toward the ceiling.

Feeling Clint's rigid shaft slide into her from that new angle was enough to send ripples of pleasure through Sofia's skin. He was rubbing against the sensitive skin of her clitoris every time he moved, and she could feel herself becoming wetter to allow him easier entry. She tightened the lips of her pussy around him when he was in all the way and kept them tight as he pulled out again. Now, it was Clint's turn to let out a deep breath and roll his eyes upward.

"Oh my god," Clint moaned.

Sofia smiled and shifted beneath him. Spreading her legs a little wider, she got her heels dug in against a step and lifted her hips up just a little bit as his body moved back. When he leaned back as far as he could go, Sofia reached out and placed her hand upon him so that her fingertips were against the bare skin of his chest.

When Clint tried to come forward, he was stopped just enough to get him to halt before moving all the way like he intended. He looked at her to see what she was doing, but got his only real answer from the motion of her hips.

Sofia kept her hand on his chest and moved her hips up and away from the stairs. The motion went like a ripple up her stomach muscles as she moved herself up along Clint's body in a serpentine fashion. While making sure Clint remained motionless, she moved her hips up and down, sliding his cock in and out of her without him having to do a thing.

Once she had her rhythm down, Clint closed his eyes and savored the feeling of her sliding back and forth against his rigid column of flesh. Even though he was on top of her, it seemed as if she were riding him, grinding her hips in perfect time so that they both could feel the pleasure of the motion.

Clint enjoyed the way she worked him for a few minutes before wanting to take back the reins and be the one in charge. This showed through in his eyes and when he looked at her that certain way, Sofia responded with an eager smile.

Once again, Clint's hands closed on top of Sofia's. This time, however, he laced his fingers between hers until he felt her hands make little fists within his own. Once he had her in his grasp, Clint moved his arms up slowly, taking her along with him.

Sofia savored the feeling of being controlled. Her eyes closed a bit and her lips parted as she reflexively lifted her face to Clint's until she could kiss him deeply and passionately. Her tongue slid between Clint's lips, mingling with his as he brought her hands up over her head. When she opened her eyes again, her arms were stretched up all the way and held in place as if she'd suddenly been taken captive.

Clint's face was intense as he moved on top of her. His erect shaft glided between the slick lips of her pussy, still pumping in and out as he got her into her new position. One of Sofia's feet bumped against the banister support she'd been grabbing earlier, making her realize that their movement had carried them up the staircase almost to the very top.

In fact, Clint's hands pressed hers down onto the uppermost step and their bodies covered a good portion of the rest. Sofia pushed the ball of her foot against that support so she could lift her other leg up and wrap it around Clint's waist.

Lowering his chest down onto her large breasts, Clint rubbed his body against hers while burying his face into the base of her neck. He was suddenly surrounded by the fragrant softness of her hair and could hear nothing but the rush of her breathy groans as he nibbled and kissed her flesh.

Something clunked against the stairs and Clint was a little surprised to see that it was his gun belt. In the course of their lovemaking, they'd managed not only to climb the stairs, but wriggle out of the rest of their clothes as well. Their bodies were completely naked by the time they got to the top and Sofia was stretched out beneath him so she could feel as much of her skin pressed against his as humanly possible.

They were also at the best spot they could be on the stairs since their bodies had completely adjusted to the angle and inclines. Now they were free to explore each other fully. Clint's body rocked back and forth on top of hers while Sofia writhed perfectly to bring the sensations to even better heights.

When she arched her back, Clint was able to move his mouth down just far enough for him to run his lips against her hard nipples. The stubble on his chin scraped against the smooth, sweaty skin between her breasts and Clint let go of her hands so he could kiss one and then the other.

Still climbing one step at a time, Sofia's backside bumped against the top step while Clint stayed right where he was. As she moved up past him, Clint didn't take his mouth off her skin once. His lips brushed against her nipples, then down over her stomach before the soft thatch of hair between her legs was less than an inch from his tongue.

Clint looked up at her, smiled, and then flicked his tongue two or three times over the swollen little pink nub of her clit. That caused Sofia to thrash against the floor, and when she recovered enough to look at him again, he was straddling her one final time. With his knees on the top step, Clint reached down to cup her generous backside in both hands and lift her up so he could slide into her even easier.

With her orgasm coming on fast, Sofia pressed both hands against the floor and thrust her hips in a quick motion until her breath was rushing through her lungs.

Clint let himself go as well and threw himself totally into the moment. He pulled almost out of her every time and slammed into her with increasing force. Every time their bodies slapped together, Sofia cried out a little louder until she was literally clawing at the floor with both hands.

Finally, they climaxed at the same time. The pleasure was so powerful that Clint nearly lost his balance before getting himself to fall forward and catch himself with both hands. For the next few moments, they stared into each other's eyes as the last tingling reminders of their orgasms faded away. Then, they hurried off into Sofia's bedroom.

NINE

It had only been a matter of hours since they'd made love on the staircase, but Clint and Sofia were so tired that it seemed they'd just gotten finished running a mile. That was understandable, however, since it was a very eventful couple of hours.

They were both in her bedroom, but the blankets on her bed were only slightly mussed. Although they'd managed to pleasure each other a few more times in those hours, most of their energy was spent by the time they'd actually reached the bed. Every other place between there and the top of the stairs had been christened.

The floor, the end tables, even a large dresser had served nicely as they continued to explore each other's bodies.

They'd spent the whole day joking with each other, discussing little things about their lives and backgrounds before the conversation inevitably led back to more basic instincts. There was an attraction between them that was purely sexual, it hooked into both of them if they made the mistake of looking at each other for too long. She'd offered to fetch him something to drink, but got up to head downstairs wearing nothing but his unbuttoned shirt. Each of them managed to take a sip of water apiece before Clint's hands were sliding over her hips and he was lifting her onto the closest table.

When he'd thought she was asleep earlier, Clint had rolled onto his back and within minutes, he felt Sofia's soft lips wrapped around his hardening cock. Even then, they hadn't stayed on the bed for too long and she'd led him to a thick fur rug where they could stretch out even more.

Now, with Sofia lying on the bed lightly sleeping, Clint walked over to the small rectangular windows looking down onto the street below. They were high enough for him to be able to see the next street over, which had more shops and should have been much busier.

Of course, "should have been" was the phrase that stuck in Clint's mind.

That other street should have been busier. It was busier the last time Clint had seen it and that was only a few hours ago. There should have been more people walking up and down the street, going from shop to shop. There should have been more wagons or horses riding along the wider avenue.

There should have been all of those things, but there simply wasn't any of them.

In fact, Clint counted only two people moving along that business district and had seen no sign of life on the street just outside Sofia's window. Despite the fact that the sun had already gone down by this time and Cielo Grande wasn't exactly a sprawling city, there still should have been more than a handful of people out and about on the crooked streets.

Clint glanced over to the clock leaning against the wall

opposite of Sofia's bed and saw that it was even a bit later than he'd thought.

"What's the matter?" Sofia's voice came from the pale light that was a combination of starlight and a single lantern. "You look like something's bothering you."

Standing with one hand on the wall, Clint turned so he could look over his shoulder at her. "I thought you were asleep."

Sofia stretched out on the bed. She was completely naked and lounged like a contented cat. The curves of her body looked magnificent in the sparse light, and it was obvious that she knew that very thing. "I was asleep, but then again I thought you might want to start something up again. I wouldn't want to miss that."

"I've got to rest sometime. That is," Clint added with a smile, "unless you were trying to kill me."

"Now, that would be one hell of a way to go." She laughed a bit at that, but sat up when she saw Clint hardly reacting at all. "Now I know something's wrong. Your sense of humor couldn't have dried up already."

Turning back toward the window, Clint said, "It's after six o'clock."

"Yeah," Sofia said after consulting the nearby clock to be sure. "Is there somewhere you needed to be?"

"No, but shouldn't other folks have places to go and things to do? What about going to get some dinner or walking to a saloon? There are saloons and restaurants here, aren't there?"

"Yes, Clint. Of course there are." Now there was some concern growing in Sofia's voice. She crawled to the edge of the bed, swung her feet over and reached out to grab a robe that was lying over the back of a padded chair.

After slipping into the robe, she tied it shut and went over to stand next to Clint. She noticed right away that he was staring intently out through the window, so Sofia looked out there as well. A full minute went by, allowing the silence in the room to become something akin to a thick fog.

Suddenly, she rubbed her arms as though she'd caught a chill. "What is it, Clint? Why won't you tell me what's wrong?"

"Nothing."

"Don't say that. I know there's something wrong, I can feel—"

"No," Clint interrupted. "Look out there and tell me what you see." After feeling around the edge of the window, Clint found the latch, turned it and let the pane swing outward on its hinges. "As a matter of fact, take a moment and listen."

He and Sofia both concentrated on what they could hear. Their eyes glazed over a bit as all their attention was diverted to their ears and every little thing they could detect. Apart from the wind and the occasional sound of an animal, there wasn't anything else for either of them to focus on.

"I don't hear anything," Sofia finally admitted.

"Exactly. Isn't that strange? This house in the middle of a street with neighbors on both sides. A larger business district is only one street over and we can't hear anything. We can't even see anyone walking around. Does this place usually get so quiet so early?"

Her eyes narrowing, Sofia finally seemed to have caught some of what had been making Clint so uneasy. "No. It doesn't."

Just as Clint was going to add something else, his eyes caught a movement coming from a trail leading into town. It was a fluke that he could see it at all since he'd been looking between two buildings that were higher than anything else up to the town's border.

What he saw was a group of horses bringing riders into town. They'd appeared as shapes breaking into his field of vision. If not for the distinctive way they moved, Clint might not have been able to tell they were horses at all. But the bouncing trot was unmistakable, especially for someone practiced in watching for anyone coming up to pay him a visit.

Now that he had something to truly focus on, Clint didn't want to lose sight of it. The path in the distance could just barely be seen, however, and soon the riders would disappear behind the building across the street. After doing some quick figuring, Clint guessed that those riders would be inside the town's limits within a couple of minutes.

"The roof," Clint said sharply. "Is there a way up to the roof?"

Although she had questions to ask, Sofia was affected by the urgency in Clint's voice. "There's a trapdoor in the attic, but there isn't anything up there but—"

"Just take me there."

Moments later, Clint and Sofia were standing on the roof of her home overlooking the rest of the town. They were just high enough to see over the neighboring buildings and beyond the limits of the town itself. Clint didn't have any trouble finding what he was looking for.

"How many men ride with Dutch?" Clint asked.

"Four. There's five of them in all."

Clint pointed toward the approaching riders. There were five of them in all.

TEN

Clint was back inside and dressed in the space of a minute or two. Sofia was right behind him, trying her best to keep up while he rushed through the house collecting his things. She tried getting his attention, but he was too distracted for the time being. Her steady stream of questions stopped, however, when Clint buckled his gun belt around his waist and checked to make sure the Colt was fully loaded.

Oddly enough, Clint took notice of her almost the second Sofia stopped talking. He dropped the Colt into its holster and looked over at her suddenly pale face. "Don't worry," he said. "It may be nothing at all."

Shaking her head, Sofia locked her eyes on Clint. "You don't seem like the type that spooks too easy. You don't think it's nothing, do you?"

For a moment, Clint considered lying to her. It would have been an easy way to try and keep her calm, but it would have been close to cheating as well. Besides, going by the look on her face, it was well past the time to calm her down quickly.

"I think I'll know more once I get down to the street,"

Clint finally told her. "It sure seems like something's spooked folks around here enough to make them head for cover."

They were standing at the bottom of the stairs and Sofia looked over toward a narrow window not too far away. She couldn't see much except for the small back lot, and when she turned around again, Clint was already walking toward the front door.

"Wait," she called out. "I want to come with you."

Without looking back, Clint answered, "No. Stay here. If that is Dutch coming back into town, I'd rather you weren't anywhere near me."

"But . . . they probably know you came back here with me. We didn't exactly hide ourselves earlier today. All Dutch would have to do is ask around and he'd know to come here."

Clint stopped just short of the door and turned around. He wasn't sure whether or not she was just bluffing to get him to change his mind. What he did know was that there was a possibility she was right and that was all he needed.

"All right," he said, opening the door. "Come with me, but watch yourself. You do what I say, when I say it. Understand?"

Sofia nodded.

"Since you know Dutch better than I do, I want you to take me to where he and his boys usually go. A favorite saloon, that type of thing. You know what I mean?"

She didn't even have to think about it for more than a second or two. "Paco's," Sofia said. "It's a place a few blocks from here. I can take you right to it."

"Who's Paco?"

"The man who owns Paco's Cantina."

Clint shook his head. "Get moving, smartass."

He wasn't happy about her coming along, but Clint

was fairly certain that if he didn't give his blessing to it, Sofia would have just followed him anyway. At least this way he could keep an eye on her better than if she was trying to lurk in the shadows.

When they got into the street, the silence that had caught Clint's attention seemed even thicker than before. The town felt even more deserted now that he was moving around inside of it instead of looking out through a window. Sofia led him through a couple shortcuts that he might have avoided if not for the fact that they seemed to be the only ones out in the night air.

Clint was reminded that the locals hadn't simply disappeared every time he glanced into a window and saw nervous faces looking intently back at him. Seeing those folks huddled close to the glass and peering out expectantly told him that there was most definitely something coming that everyone wanted to avoid.

Everyone, that is, except for those who charged right out so they could find it.

After crossing a few streets and cutting through some alleyways, Clint and Sofia emerged in a section of town that actually seemed to have some life in it. There still wasn't much by way of movement, and the only reason Clint had missed it before was that it was on the wrong side of a building that blocked his view from Sofia's house.

A few drunks wandered around the street, trying to get to the next saloon before they collapsed. Here and there, working girls stood in doorways, beckoning to the few potential customers who crossed their paths. But these weren't the ones who caught Clint's attention.

The one figure that interested him the most was a skinny runt of a man who darted from one doorway to another. He would poke his head in or speak quickly to someone standing nearby before running off to wherever he was going. In several respects, that skinny runt reminded Clint of the kid who'd been spreading the news earlier in the day.

Just as he started running again, the runt noticed Clint looking at him and started to turn and head in the other direction. But it was too late for that maneuver, and his steps had already brought him within Clint's arm's reach.

With a motion that was swift and sure, Clint reached out to snag the runt's elbow. The smaller man tried to run but quickly found himself being snapped back like a dog who'd raced all the way to the end of its leash.

"What's going on?" Clint asked.

The running man squinted in concentration even though he was close enough for the stink of his breath to wash all over both Clint and Sofia.

Since he didn't recognize either one of them, he shook his head and stammered, "N . . . nothin'. Nothin'. I ain't doin' nothin'."

"Take it easy. Just tell me what you've been telling everyone else."

"What I been telling? You mean you ain't heard? Dutch Dreyman is headed this way and he's brought every one of his boys with him." Before Clint could say anything, the drunk added, "You don't believe me? Then look for yerself!"

Clint turned and felt the drunk pull himself away at his first opportunity. Letting the other man go, Clint made sure he knew where Sofia was and then positioned himself between her and the five men who rode slowly toward the cantina.

"Get inside," Clint told her. "Find someplace out of the way and stay there. This might just get ugly."

ELEVEN

From what he'd seen of Dutch, Clint knew the other man was short-tempered and quick to go for a gun. Although that didn't make him the most dangerous man in the land, it did make him trouble to folks who might be standing around nearby. Not wanting to put any bystanders in danger, Clint moved to the only place where his back wasn't to a building full of people.

The street was deserted and Clint stood right in the middle of it, facing the approaching riders. As long as he could believe what Sofia had told him, Dutch had all of his boys with him and there weren't any more skulking about trying to sneak up on him.

All the better for Clint.

Not so good for Dutch.

The silence was almost complete. Apart from the calm wind, the only thing to be heard was the crunch of hooves upon packed dirt. That sound grew louder as the five men got closer. Finally, the man in the middle raised his hand and brought his horse to a stop. The other four followed suit, taking up positions around the middle figure like some kind of ragged honor guard.

It took a few moments for Clint's eyes to adjust to the darkness after looking into the cantina to check on Sofia. Fortunately, Dutch was so confident in what he thought was a frightening presence, he gave Clint more than enough time to prepare.

"Is that really you, Dutch?" Clint asked, playing up the notion that he couldn't see into the shadows too well.

Dutch nodded and let a smirk creep up beneath his scraggly mustache and beard. "Yeah, it's me. Who the hell did you think it was?"

"I don't know. I guess I didn't think you'd be back so soon after getting run out of here earlier today."

Even in the darkness, Clint could see the flash of anger that washed over Dutch's face. The men on either side of him glanced around like they didn't quite know how to react. Obviously, not a lot of people talked to Dutch Dreyman that way.

Dutch was in such a hurry to get down from his horse that he spooked the animal in his clumsy scramble toward the ground. Managing to land with both feet on the ground, Dutch took a few steps forward. The other four men looked as if they meant to follow, but kept from doing so. Instead, they stayed in their saddles and kept a few paces behind Dutch as he walked forward.

That was enough to make Clint sure that Dutch had planned this out at least a little. The others were supposed to stay on horseback while Dutch went in on his own. He had to grin at how brave Dutch seemed to feel having not only four men, but four horses behind him as backup.

"What the hell are you smiling at?" Dutch snarled. "I don't recall sayin' anything funny."

Once again, Clint squinted at Dutch. "You know what's funny? I swear I see guns on you and your boys back there."

"So?"

"I thought I made it clear you weren't supposed to carry guns here anymore."

"Let me make somethin' clear to you," Dutch said. "I do whatever the hell I want and nobody tells me any different. You got lucky earlier. That's all. And if you weren't such a smartass, I might have just let you go. But that ain't gonna happen. Not no more."

Clint could see faces peeking out from every window facing the street. They glimpsed from behind curtains that were held open just enough for them to get a somewhat decent view. They were all petrified, but not one of them looked away.

"All right," Clint finally said. "Maybe I have been a little rude. If I have, then I apologize. How's that?"

For a moment, Dutch looked at him in a way that reminded Clint of a confused dog. "That ain't good enough."

"Then what do you want? Surely you must have come riding back in here for something."

"Yeah. I came here because there ain't nobody supposed to wear guns in my town 'cept for me and my boys."

"Well I'm not from around here."

"I heard that. You're Clint Adams. Big-time Gunsmith, and just because of that, we're all supposed to run scared. Is that it?"

"Not at all. In fact, this can all just blow over and you can buy your boys all the drinks they can stomach. But if you want to start making policy, run for mayor. If you don't get elected, then shut the hell up."

TWELVE

The silence that filled the next couple of seconds was heavier than a shroud. Dutch glared at Clint, but got nothing more than a blank stare in return.

"You know what?" Dutch said. "I was ready to get a drink and then tear this town apart looking for you. I was even looking forward to that part. And even though you were kind enough to show up right away, I think I'll let my boys tear some things up anyhow. They've earned it, and folks need to be reminded who calls the shots around here."

Turning to glance over his shoulder, Dutch lifted one hand and waved forward. "Go on, boys. Show everyone why it ain't healthy to piss me off while I take care of Mister Gunsmith over here. Hell, killing this asshole won't just be fun, it'll make me famous to boot!"

All four of the men behind Dutch started to holler at the top of their lungs like a bunch of wild animals. They got their horses moving and snatched their guns from their holsters. Without even taking a moment to aim, they started firing wildly in all directions. Bullets whipped through the air. Glass shattered and screams could be heard from some of the nearby buildings.

Waiting for the commotion to reach its peak, Dutch went for his gun. While he might have thought Clint would be even a little distracted by all the ruckus, he was too busy making his move to see that Clint hadn't moved or taken his eyes off of him.

Not even a little.

So much was happening around him. Guns were blazing and lead flew every which way but Sunday, but Clint's mind had already sped up to make up for it all. The only things that he took notice of were those that were vitally important.

He knew a distraction when he saw one, and figured that that had been Dutch's plan all along. Despite the victorious smile on Dutch's face, Clint had to admit that it was one of the most piss-poor plans he'd ever seen.

That smug grin was on Dutch's face as he slid the gun out of his holster. Actually, he almost got the gun out of the holster before Clint's hand flashed down to wrap around his Colt. Clint had cleared leather and taken his shot before Dutch's finger was all the way around his trigger.

Clint's shot could barely be heard over all the fire being laid down by Dutch's boys. But even without being heard above everything else, Clint's single bullet was the only one to damage something besides a window or wall.

The chunk of lead hissed through the air and drilled a hole clean through Dutch's chest. Dutch was still in the process of drawing his weapon when he felt the sudden, stabbing pain.

Confused, Dutch kept trying to draw, but he no longer had the strength. In fact, he couldn't lift his arm and couldn't even stay on his feet any longer. Before he knew what was going on, he'd dropped to the ground and was blinking up at the sky as his entire world started fading into black.

It happened so quickly that Dutch's boys didn't even know what was going on. As far as they knew, the original plan was still in effect and going just fine. After the prescribed amount of time went by, all four of the remaining gunmen turned toward Clint and swung their guns around to take aim.

As soon as he knew he'd put Dutch down, Clint had turned his attention to the other four. He was just in time to see them adjust their aim so they were targeting him and not just anything they could lay their eyes on. Clint didn't waste a moment in thinking about what he should do. Instead, he handed himself over to his instincts and let his body move where they told him to go.

The ground rumbled beneath Clint's feet as two of the horses started coming straight for him. He dove forward with both hands extended, twisting his body in midair so he landed on his shoulder rather than his face or chest. He hit the ground hard, but kept the wind from getting knocked out of him. Still turning to keep the horsemen in his sight, Clint saw the closest one was swiveling in the saddle to bring his gun around.

Jim was the name of the man who had Clint in his sights. At least, he'd thought Clint was in his sights. Actually, he had another half-second to go before he could line his aim up properly and that was more time than Clint needed to take a shot of his own.

This time, there weren't other shots competing with the thunder from Clint's modified Colt. The pistol roared once and spat its round through the air. Jim spun in his saddle and fell off his horse, landing with a jarring thud. Blood from the fresh wound in his side poured into the dirt.

Wanting to keep surprise on his side, Clint did the last thing he figured the horsemen would expect and jumped to his feet. When Jim's horse cleared the way, Clint was standing tall in front of a water trough rather than hiding behind it.

The sight of him there must have surprised the others indeed, because they came up short and took on a shocked expression. The other three had their guns in hand, but were pointing them skyward.

Clint stood his ground, smoking Colt in hand, and waited for the men to make their move. If they wanted to run, he intended on letting them go. If they wanted to fight, he intended on granting that wish as well. The only thing he wasn't ready to do was let them keep raising hell in a town that was sick to death of acting as their playground.

The remaining three seemed to sense what Clint was giving them. Even though Dutch was lying dead in the street, the others were still looking to him as though expecting more orders. When none came, they each had to make up their own mind.

One of them was apparently a quicker thinker than the others.

With his neatly parted hair blowing in the night breeze, Andy straightened his arm so he could sight down his barrel at Clint. A nasty snarl twisted his smooth features and his finger tightened around his trigger.

Clint only had to move a select few muscles as he turned his Colt slightly up to compensate for the new angle and fired once from the hip. The bullet he'd set loose slapped against Andy's skull, knocked his head back and sped out through his neatly parted hair.

For a moment, Andy still looked down his barrel at Clint. Then his eyes glazed over and his mouth dropped open before he fell sideways off his horse. Jim, who was barely hanging on to consciousness, tried to push himself back so he didn't have to be so close to the fresh corpse that landed beside him.

That left two more on horseback. Each looked quickly over to the other before tossing their guns away and steering their horses back in the direction they'd come. They made it less than a quarter of the way down the street when they were stopped by a line of gray-haired men blocking their path.

"Get the hell out of our way!" one of the riders shouted. Some of the steam left his voice halfway through the demand when he realized he was no longer armed. The next thing he was about to say stuck in his throat when he realized that every one of the old men were carrying shotguns.

One of the old men had long, silvery hair hanging down well past his shoulders. When Clint got a look at him, the man reminded him of what Wild Bill might have looked like if he'd lived fifteen or twenty more years.

"Get down off those horses before I cut you down where you sit!" the old man shouted.

After not too much deliberation, both of the riders came down and immediately threw their hands in the air as soon as their boots hit the dirt.

Clint walked over to the men who were lying on the ground as he replaced the spent shells in his Colt's cylinder. Andy and Dutch were dead. Jim was clutching a nasty wound in his side, but would probably pull through. The other two were being rounded up by the old men who'd taken it upon themselves to finally take a stand.

"Well," Clint thought. "Better late than never."

Holstering the Colt, Clint walked over to the old men and made sure to keep his hands where they could be seen. Getting to the pistol in time wasn't a concern in his mind. Getting on the wrong side of those shotgunners, on the other hand, was a whole other story.

"You can put them hands down," the old man with the Wild Bill look about him said. "I know who you are and I seen what you done this morning."

"I was hoping they'd leave and stay gone," Clint said. "But since they came back, I thought I'd head them off before anyone got hurt."

"Some broken glass and such, but nobody's hurt. At least," the old man added, glancing toward Andy and Dutch, "nobody that matters." He extended a hand and walked forward with the shotgun held in the crook of his other arm. "Name's Samuel Bowdrie."

"Pleasure's mine. What do you do around here, Sam?"

"Carpenter."

"You ask me, that should make for a nice hobby if you still have the time. A man like you should be doing this town a service."

"Like something more than risking my neck out here?"

"Like being its sheriff."

Bowdrie huffed at that and then nodded. "Sheriff, huh?" he grumbled. "I like the sound of that."

THIRTEEN

Now, three years later, Clint let a little smile form on his face. It was just a reaction to what had happened and how he'd reacted. All in all, apart from having the lead thrown his way, things had gone pretty well. And there wasn't a bad thing he could possibly think about with regard to his time with Sofia.

But what he smiled about was more of a sense of accomplishment. The feeling of a job well done. He'd made a difference in Cielo Grande and that wasn't the type of thing every man could say when they visited a place for the first time. The town was better for him having been there.

Clint had tipped the balance.

By the time he'd ridden out of town, Cielo Grande had a new sheriff and its locals didn't have to watch themselves around a temperamental bully who might just shoot at them for sport. The town even had a better feel to it. In a way, it felt as if the very air itself was lighter and easier to breathe.

Then why did he still have the feeling that there was something wrong? Why did he have a strange discomfort in his gut that something important was missing or out of place?

So far, the town seemed pretty much the same. Surely there were some changes that had taken place since he'd left, but nothing that should make him uneasy. In fact, the buildings seemed to be in better shape and the boardwalks didn't sag dangerously between the studs.

The more he felt that gnawing in his belly, the more his smile started to fade. His eyes shifted back and forth as he rode down the street, looking for something to justify the way he was feeling. As bad as it sounded, he would have felt better if there had been something obviously wrong with the place. At least that way he would have a reason for this odd sensation.

Clint was almost to the row of shops where he'd first met up with Dutch and his boys. By this time, he was beginning to feel foolish for fussing over what—as far as he could tell—might have been nothing at all. Perhaps that odd feeling in his stomach was just leftover nerves. After all, he did get shot at last time he was in town, and he'd been forced to put three men into their graves.

Unfortunately, that wasn't a very rare occurrence. Clint had been shot at in plenty of towns and had put many men in their graves. He also felt uneasy about them as well. No matter how bad a man might have been, killing him would leave the survivor changed. That was just the way it went. That was the price for having a soul.

Right about now was when Clint noticed the number of people walking down the street. There weren't as many as he remembered, but that could be due to a great number of things. Since he was getting tired of trying to figure this thing out, Clint decided to just get a room for the night and buy himself a nice steak dinner. Perhaps that feeling was just hunger and would stop nagging him once some meat was thrown into the mix.

Clint did just that. He passed a hotel and took note of where it was in the back of his mind. From there, he went to the first restaurant he could find, which was a place called. Dalton's Chop House. The place was about half full and served a fine steak. According to Dalton, a chubby man with a round, red face, a cattle drive had passed through not too long ago and he'd managed to get a few head of cattle for himself.

With his belly full, Clint was feeling much better. For a moment, he thought that hunger had been his only problem after all. But that contentment didn't last too long, and soon the sense of uneasiness came back again.

Focusing on what else needed to be done, Clint rode to the livery, which was still in the same place he remembered from the last time he was there. Plenty of stalls were available and the moment he saw the inside of the place, Clint remembered who'd run it three years ago.

"Does Marc Abels still own this place?" Clint asked the small-boned young woman who took Eclipse's reins.

She looked at him as though he'd tried to bark at her before nodding once. Her wiry brown hair was pulled back into two ponytails. She had a face that might have been a whole lot prettier if she'd bothered taking care of herself. Smiling a bit wouldn't have hurt either. "Sure does. You hear anything different?"

"No. Just asking."

"He'll be in tomorrow if you want to talk to him. Did I do something wrong?"

"No, I wasn't going to complain. I just . . ." Clint let his sentence trail off when he could see that she was no longer listening. The young woman was still standing in the same spot, but she was looking at Eclipse. Only when she started brushing the Darley Arabian's mane did her features brighten and her mannerism soften just a bit.

At least Eclipse would have good company for the night.

"All right then," Clint said as a formality more than any real attempt to communicate. "I'll get going. The name's Clint Adams. If you could, let Marc know I'm here." He waited for a reply of any sort. When he didn't get one, he asked, "Could you do that for me? Please?"

She nodded, but Clint doubted seriously that she would remember what he'd asked. If not for the stallion he'd left in her care, he doubted she would remember he was there at all.

Clint walked out of the stables, confident that Eclipse was going to be well cared for. Besides that, he had a full stomach and had the night free to spend as he wanted. Plenty of men would have killed for a night like that, but Clint still couldn't shake the uneasy feeling in the pit of his stomach.

Stepping onto the street that led to the saloon district, Clint looked down to the end of the block as well as the next block over when he turned the corner. That vague uneasiness was still present like a constant humming in the back of his head.

This time, however, it was stronger. Maybe it was due to all the thinking he'd just been doing about the last time he'd been there, but he felt as though he'd only been gone for perhaps a few months. Walking in the same tracks that had been in his memories helped jog his brain a little more, so that's what he did.

He walked toward the saloons while his eyes hunted for whatever it was that had gotten under his skin.

FOURTEEN

There was a building missing.

When Clint turned the corner on his way to the saloon district, he spotted the empty lot immediately. At that moment, the gnawing in his stomach ended and the nagging in his brain finally came to a stop.

That was why he'd felt something was off when he'd looked at the town from afar. That was why he felt that there was something strange about the place when he'd ridden in and wandered the streets.

The last time he was in Cielo Grande, there had been a large building two floors high that had been a significant part of the skyline. When he closed his eyes, he could almost see the town the way it had been. Clint's memory was anything but perfect, but he knew that he'd recognized that hole where a rooftop should have been.

In a strange way, he felt happy to have finally put his finger on what had eluded him since his arrival. Unfortunately, that happiness lasted right up until he got close enough to see the entire vacant lot that used to have been filled by his missing building.

The lot wasn't simply vacant, and it didn't look as

though something had been knocked over to make room for something else. The lot was a blackened hole, which still smelled like rotten wood, soot and mold. It was coated with dark ash and the charred remnants of furniture and other items that hadn't been pulled out in time to be saved from the blaze.

Clint stood there looking at the remains of the building, letting his eyes wander over the damage. From the looks of it, nobody had even tried to clean much of anything away. Broken chairs were lying in front of gutted shells that used to be a roll-top desk and various sizes of cabinets.

Jagged chunks of walls were still rooted to the ground in other areas, as were heaps of rubble, which were once the upper floor and ceiling. Some piles were bigger than others and Clint could tell that it was just the randomness of the fire that had decided the sizes. Some areas burned more intensely, and those were the areas where he could see down to the scorched earth.

Other areas had either been doused by frantic townspeople forming a water brigade or possibly the fire had just been snuffed by falling debris. One thing was for sure, no effort had been made to clear any of the rubble away. This was how it had looked as soon as the fire had been put out. Any other adjustments to the wreckage were made by the weather.

That was the only way to explain why there was mold growing on some of the burned pieces of furniture. Looking closer, Clint was able to spot things like coatracks and even a couple rifles lying in the ash that could have been picked up, cleaned off and used again. There were even things of a more personal nature like picture frames and a fancy belt buckle lying not too far from where Clint was standing.

Metal pieces on those items were rusted over and the soot was so thick and settled that it appeared to be more like a crust that had been baked onto everything else. All of this told Clint that somebody had purposely avoided cleaning up this mess. It also told him that the mess had been there for quite a while.

Before he realized it, several minutes had passed and Clint was still standing at the edge of the burned-out building. His feet remained where they were, as if they'd been planted on that spot. There was something about the building's remains that seemed so fresh and yet so old.

The contrast was striking, and it only grew the longer he looked at it. Without too much concentration, Clint could practically hear the crackling of the flames that had consumed this place. He could hear things worse than that if he thought about it any longer, which was why he forced himself to look away.

All around him, people walked by as if they were completely used to the idea of living with the charred skeleton of a building. They didn't even look at him too strangely for standing there staring at the place. The locals only seemed to act strangely when Clint tried getting their attention.

At first, when he asked for a moment of someone's time, the person seemed ready to talk to Clint. That stopped as soon as they saw where he was standing and guessed about what his question would be. It wasn't until he saw an elderly couple walking his way that Clint found anyone willing to stop and speak to him.

"Excuse me," Clint said to the couple who walked hand in hand down the street. "What happened here?"

"Can't you see?" the old man said, gesturing toward the wreckage with one sweeping hand. "Place burnt down."

"What used to be here?"

The old man paused and looked around. When he saw that there weren't too many people nearby, he replied, "The sheriff's office."

FIFTEEN

Clint had to take another look for himself.

Even though he'd seen enough to scorch the sight onto his brain for a good long while, he had to look again now that he knew what had once stood in that blackened, dirty hole. As he did, he thought about Samuel Bowdrie who'd taken it upon himself to gather up some men and come help Clint the night he'd faced down Dutch Dreyman.

Sure, that help hadn't come until the hard work was done, but it was a hell of a lot more than anyone else had been willing to do. Besides that, Clint had gotten the sense that Bowdrie would have been there sooner if he hadn't had to collect others to stand beside him.

That was all just gut feelings on Clint's part, but he tended to trust them anyhow. His gut usually led him in the right direction. It certainly had this time around.

Turning back toward the elderly couple, Clint asked, "When did this . . . ?" But there was no need to finish the question. The couple had already moved on. Even though they hadn't gotten very far, it was plain to see by the quickness in their steps that they didn't want to talk anymore.

Clint wanted to walk away from the sight, but it held him there, and he couldn't get himself to leave. There was just so much to see within the ash. So many shapes that seemed like one thing and then turned out to be something else.

There were pieces of broken wood which turned out to be an overturned chair. Subtle glints of light off metal revealed bullet casings or even items that would be found in a man's pocket. Most of these things were damaged or destroyed, while others were dirty, but in surprisingly good shape.

Just when Clint thought he'd seen enough, his eyes wandered to the remains of the structure itself. He wondered how so much of one wall could be standing when certain sections were nothing more than piles of black rubble. There were even one or two places where the interior of the building could be seen; doorways that were still standing and even one part of a wall with a square hole where there'd been a window.

It was the smell of the ash that caused Clint to turn away. He couldn't be sure how long the building had been left like that, but there was still enough black dust being kicked up to coat the inside of his nose. When he cleared his throat, he could taste the ash as though he'd been one of the men to put out the initial blaze.

When his back was turned to the burned-out sheriff's office, Clint saw that nobody walking along the street was looking at him or the building. He got the feeling that they could see him just fine, but were avoiding making eye contact for some reason.

This made Clint want to take the people by the shoulders as they walked by and shake them. The more eyes that didn't turn his way, the more his frustration grew.

What he felt wasn't the type of frustration that had anger attached, but a certain kind of tiredness.

He'd seen that sort of purposeful ignorance before. In fact, he'd seen some of that in those same streets only three years ago. Thinking along those lines, Clint couldn't help but wonder if this wasn't somehow connected to what he'd done back then.

Was the fire set by more of Dutch's boys who hadn't been there to see Clint's last night in town? Or was it part of some kind of jailbreak to free the men that Sam Bowdrie had captured?

There wasn't any way Clint was going to answer those questions by staring at burned walls, so he started walking across the street and continued on his way to a saloon. Some beer would go a long way in helping to wash away the taste of fire that still lingered in his throat. Besides, folks were always more apt to talk in a saloon.

Clint hadn't taken three steps when he noticed that one of the locals he'd spotted wasn't averting her eyes after all. In fact, not only weren't they looking away, but those eyes were aimed straight at him and staying there.

The woman had the face of someone in her early to mid-twenties, but her eyes were filled with a certain something that made her look a bit older. Clint had seen eyes like that before and they were usually owned by people who'd seen more than they would have liked. With what he knew about Cielo Grande, Clint wasn't at all surprised.

She stepped forward when she knew Clint had spotted her. "It's a damn shame."

"You've got that right," Clint replied once he walked up a little closer. "Mind if I ask what happened here?"

Her smile was pretty, but more than a little wary. "A fire," was all she said to answer the question.

"That's all anyone seems to say about it."

"I know. It's a damn shame."

SIXTEEN

She wore a simple tan cotton dress with a wrap over her shoulders that had light and dark brown stripes. The earth tones of her clothes made the blond color of her hair seem to take on more of a brilliant golden hue. Her skin appeared touched by the sun as well, but only slightly, and when Clint got close enough, he could see the hazel in her eyes.

"You're new in town," she said without a doubt in her mind. "And my guess is you've never been here before, either."

"I am new, but I've passed through here before. Three years ago, actually."

"Ah. Well, I was close. Anyway, do yourself a favor and pretend like that eyesore isn't even there. You'll blend in much better with these people."

Despite the fact that the others passing by were trying to ignore Clint, he definitely picked up some reaction on the nearby faces when the blonde said that last part.

It wasn't good.

She apparently noticed this as well and shot the offended passersby with a look of her own, which made them continue on their way all the faster. When she looked back at Clint, although she still wasn't in the brightest of spirits, her face looked sunny in comparison to the one she'd shown just a second ago.

"There's a nice place to stay just down this road and around the corner," she told him. "It's got a nice view."

"Really? A view of what?"

"Not this. It's called Casa Verde and it's on—"

"Mesa Street," Clint said, finishing her sentence. "That's where I stayed the last time I was here."

She nodded crisply and said, "Good. Then you already know the way. Try not to draw so much attention to yourself while you're here. Things will go much smoother for you that way."

With that, the blonde turned on her heels and started to walk away. It was all Clint could do to catch up to her before she left him in her dust. Dodging a pair of oncoming locals before knocking them over, Clint managed to get alongside the blonde so he could match her pace.

"I thought you said you knew the way," she said without looking over at him.

Clint widened his strides, which allowed him to keep up with her without having to seem like he was in a rush. "I do know the way."

"Then why aren't you headed there? You should have turned in the other direction."

"Because I've already got a room."

Shaking her head, the blonde tried to sound frustrated with him even though she couldn't hide the fact that she was smiling just a little. "My mother told me not to talk to strangers," she grumbled. "Now I know why."

"Come on," Clint chided. "You think I'm a little amusing." He waited for a few seconds and then asked in a vaguely disappointed voice, "Maybe just a little?"

"Not really."

"I see you smiling."

"The sun's in my eyes."

"The sun isn't that bright," Clint responded.

"Then maybe I just thought of something funny, like you tripping over a loose board."

"That's not funny. That's just mean for you to want me to—" but the rest of Clint's words were snagged in the back of his throat when he felt his left foot slide forward and his entire body wobble dangerously close to falling completely over.

The board he'd stepped on wasn't just loose; it wasn't even nailed down. His heel slid down the front half of the board, which had tilted down beneath his weight. The back half of the board swung up and knocked him on the back of the leg just as Clint's foot smacked against the dirt beneath the walkway.

It was only a drop of a foot or so, but Clint felt as though he'd fallen about ten yards. There was a sting in his knees, but that wasn't quite as bad as the sting he felt when he started struggling to pull his foot out of that damn hole in the boardwalk. So much for the improvements he thought he'd noticed.

"See," the blonde said. "Now, that was funny."

"Yeah. Ha ha. You think you could give me a hand here?"

She struggled to keep her amusement down to a tolerable level as she fished Clint out of the hole. He was standing on steadier ground in a few seconds, and when he set his foot back onto a firmer plank, the loose one dropped right back into place.

"Did you hurt anything?" she asked, still holding on to his arm.

He rolled his eyes and laughed a little bit, himself.

"Just my pride. No wonder you can spot newcomers so easily. With this kind of treatment, I'll bet you don't get a whole lot of them."

Clint had purposely put some agitation in his voice, hoping to get more of a reaction out of the blonde. Even though she wasn't buying into it, she walked voluntarily into the guilt trap he'd put out in front of her.

"You're right," she said. "That was mean of me. How about if I try to make it up to you?"

"That would be nice. What did you have in mind?"

"I thought I'd let you buy me a drink."

They'd started walking again and were far enough away from what was left of the sheriff's office for the people around them to act more normally. But Clint hardly noticed any of them. The more time he spent with the blond woman, the more he didn't mind blocking everybody else out completely.

"Is that how it works here?" he asked, still playing along with her. "And what would I have to do for you to buy me a drink?"

"I don't know. Maybe walk into a pole?"

Clint stopped instantly and snapped his head around so he could look where he was about to step. There wasn't a pole in his path, but when he turned around there was a wide, beautiful smile on the blonde's face. That was certainly worth the more puzzled looks he was getting from everyone else.

SEVENTEEN

Strangely enough, the place that the blond woman decided to go for her drink was Paco's Cantina. The last time he'd been in town, Clint hadn't actually gone to Paco's, but had merely waited outside of it for Dutch Dreyman to find him. Now that he was inside the place, he had to admit that it wasn't quite what he'd been expecting.

Paco's was surprisingly clean. The floors were swept and the tables were arranged in neat rows with three small chairs around each one. It was a bit early for the place to be filled, but there was a fair number of people scattered here and there, each of which kept their voices down to a respectable level.

A bar took up one corner and was tended by a Mexican with a round body and face wearing an apron that only had a few dots to smudge its otherwise snow-white color. He had his sleeves rolled up and his thick black hair cut short. A beaming smile never left his face as he made his way from one customer to another.

"Did you come here the last time you were in town?" the blonde asked Clint.

"Yes, but I didn't come inside."

She looked at him kind of funny, but kept whatever she was thinking to herself. "Paco," she called out to the bartender. "Two beers, please."

The fat man fixed his eyes on her and gave a quick salute. *"Sí, señorita. Dos cervezas."*

Clint reached out to pull out a chair for her, but the blonde walked up to the bar instead. She stood at a section that was relatively empty and waited for him to follow. When he took up a spot beside her, Clint only had to wait a second or two before she stepped close enough to him that their hips almost touched.

"So what do I have to do for you to tell me your name?" he asked her. "Trip and fall through a window?"

When she laughed, all of the tension that had been on her face melted away, and she even had to take a breath before she could answer him. "My name's Jennifer Reid."

"Clint Adams. It's a pleasure meeting you. A little hard on my knees, but a pleasure all the same."

"Clint Adams?" she repeated with an amused look and raised eyebrows. "That's awful brash."

"What?"

"If you're going to try and impress me with a famous name, the least you could do is find out where you are before picking one."

Clint didn't even try to hide his confusion. "Sorry you don't like that name, but it's the only one I've got."

Jennifer looked at him carefully. At first, her expression was disbelieving. The longer she studied Clint's face, however, the more she started to come around. "You're serious? You're really Clint Adams?"

"I take it you've heard of me."

"Heard of you?" She stopped herself quickly, looked around and started again in a lower tone of voice. "Heard of you? Everyone here's heard of you." This time, Jennifer wasn't only studying Clint's expression but every inch of his face. When she reached out to place a finger on the side of his chin so she could turn his head to the right, she gasped slightly and pulled her hand back.

"That scar," she said quietly. "It really is you."

"Like I told you the first time. Are we ready to move on to another topic or do I have to answer questions now too?"

"I'm sorry. I didn't mean to be so rude. It's just that there are a lot of stories going around about you in this town. Some of them . . . well . . . let's just say some of them aren't too flattering."

"Yeah," Clint said. "I'm not surprised."

"But most of them come from people not too many folks around here believe anyway. The stories that we can believe are still pretty fantastic."

"Well how about filling me in on what everyone's saying about me?" Clint suggested. Before Jennifer could start in on her stories, Paco came back with the beers and set them on the bar in front of them. Clint reflexively kept his face away from the Mexican and immediately felt foolish for doing so. "First, let's get ourselves a table where we can have a bit of privacy."

"Sounds like a good idea."

Jennifer seemed more relieved than the situation warranted, but Clint didn't ask about that just yet. Instead, he followed her to a small table away from the bar. He pulled out a chair for her and took one that put his own back to the wall where he could also watch the people coming and going through the front door.

After taking a sip or two of beer, Jennifer started telling Clint about the things she'd heard about him. Apart from the normal stories that were circulating about him that came from the normal sources, she had plenty of things to say about more specific happenings.

To be precise, she focused on the last time he'd been in town and what had happened when he confronted Dutch Dreyman and the gunmen who rode with him. For the most part, her retelling of those events was fairly accurate. Sure, there were some colorful details thrown in, but not enough to taint the story as a whole.

Her description of the night that Clint and Dutch fought outside the cantina was so vivid, that it sounded as though she might have been there to see it for herself. There were some inaccuracies, but those even showed up in accounts told by genuine eyewitnesses. Clint was pleased to see that at least the inaccuracies favored him in this particular story.

"Were you there that night?" he finally had to ask.

Jennifer shook her head. "No, but I was living here in town. I wasn't about to become one of those fools who runs out to take a look when they hear yelling and shooting. That's a good way to get yourself hurt."

"It's too bad that more people don't think that way."

"I think I got a look at you one time back then, but it wasn't much more than a glance. Folks around here were talking so much that you'd have thought that you were the second coming." When she said that, Jennifer looked at Clint in a different way. There wasn't the wariness or disbelief that had been there before. On the contrary, her eyes were filled with genuine admiration.

Jennifer's hands had worked their way across the top of the table until she was just about close enough to touch Clint's fingers. She didn't reach out that extra bit, however. Instead, she lowered her eyes as though she'd caught herself right before doing something she might regret and pulled her hands back to wrap around her own beer mug.

"Now don't get me wrong," she continued. "Dutch was a bastard and a killer who got what was coming to him. You did this town one hell of a service by putting him in the ground."

Clint never did like hearing about gunfights described that way. Even when he was in the damned things and his life was on the line, he still felt a pinch in his chest when someone spoke so glowingly about a scuffle where a man had lost his life.

It didn't matter who had what coming or what the dead man had done in the past. Dead was dead and that life was gone because Clint had taken it from him. That was the cause of the familiar pain he felt, and that pain never lessened over time. He took another pull from his beer to try and dull it a little.

It didn't help. It never did.

"But you already know about all of this," Jennifer said, referring to the stories she'd been telling. "What you need to know is what happened after you left. That's when things really got interesting."

EIGHTEEN

What Clint found somewhat peculiar was that Jennifer didn't seem as uncomfortable talking about the aftermath of his fight with Dutch as she had when discussing the fight itself. She obviously wasn't about to shout her story from the rooftops, but there was a definite easiness in her voice that hadn't been there before.

Her eyes locked on Clint as though they were the only two people in the room. As she talked, Jennifer ran her fingers through her long blond hair, occasionally twirling the ends before letting it fall back onto her shoulders.

"First of all," she said, "Samuel Bowdrie was elected sheriff almost unanimously. There were a few other men who stepped up to try for the job, but it was plain to see that they weren't suited for it. Hell," she added with a laugh, "nobody but Sam had the sand to come out until after the smoke cleared."

Hearing that brought a picture of Sam Bowdrie into distinct focus within Clint's mind. He could see every wrinkle on the old man's face, and it struck him even more how much the long-haired Bowdrie resembled Wild Bill. What stuck out in his mind even more was the determination in the old-timer's eyes. Bowdrie might have been afraid of getting shot, but he wasn't about to let any of those gunmen just up and run.

That was real bravery.

"He seemed like a good man," Clint said.

Jennifer nodded without hesitation. "He was. And he made a damn good sheriff. All the men that came out there with him were deputies, and he even gave jobs to the others who'd run for sheriff. I've lived in a few other towns before, but I've never seen deputies more eager to make their rounds.

"Even though Sam never was the overly anxious type, you'd have to be blind not to see that he loved his job. After what you did to Dutch, there weren't many others too eager to stir up any trouble. But even once things settled down, Sam kept the peace." Her eye twitched just a little when she added, "Yessir. He did a damn fine job."

Clint was awfully good at reading people. But, to use the phrase that Jennifer herself had said only moments ago, he would have had to have been blind not to see that something was chewing her up on the inside. Although he almost hated to ask, Clint steeled himself and moved ahead anyway.

"Jennifer, what happened to Sam?"

For a second or two, she looked as though she hadn't even heard Clint's question. But then the corners of her eyes twitched a bit more and she took a slow, quiet breath. "He . . . uhh . . ." She stopped for a second so she could quickly swipe at the corner of her eye. The way she reached up and dabbed made it seem as though she might have been embarrassed to be seen in such a way.

Blinking a few times, she looked straight at Clint and strengthened herself enough to move on as well. "He was doing a fine job, just like I said. It was quiet for a little over a year before there was any trouble at all. Even that was mostly just some cowboys passing through trying to make some noise, or a kid trying to stir up some trouble just for the hell of it. By the way folks were still talking, one might have thought you were still watching over this town."

She smiled a bit at that and she looked so sweet that Clint had to smile as well. But the moment she lowered her eyes to take a drink, the ghost that had been haunting her returned to darken her face and eyes.

"I was working at the dress shop," she went on to say. "I still am, actually. Sitting there doing fittings for all the ladies in town, I got to hear enough gossip that I wished I'd gone deaf a few times just to get away from it. That's how I heard about Brandon Morris."

The name struck Clint as something he should have recognized. But like a fly buzzing just out of his reach, it jumped around in his thoughts without ever coming to rest.

"Maybe you've heard of him?" Jennifer asked, as if she could see what was going on inside Clint's head. "He's a gunfighter from El Paso. At least, he says he's a gunfighter. Maybe it's stupid to think you would have ever crossed paths with him."

"Actually, I might have," Clint said. "I'm not sure, but the name does sound familiar."

"Well, I was doing an alteration for Miss Havermeyer's Sunday dress when she started talking about her son. This boy's been gone for years and she usually cursed every time she mentioned his name. This time, though, she seemed to talk fondly of him. That's when I knew something was wrong.

"Apparently, her boy was trying to make a name for himself as a bad man or some kind of bank robber when he hooked up with Brandon Morris. Miss Havermeyer got a letter from her son saying that he was coming to visit her, but he wouldn't be able to stay."

Jennifer picked up her beer and nearly drained the mug before going on. "The next thing she heard from him was when he showed up on her doorstep at some ungodly hour with some stranger. That stranger was Brandon Morris, and he damn near made her rich by paying for himself and all his boys to stay there.

"She told me she thought she might be found dead somewhere if Brandon and those roughnecks stayed on. But after a few weeks, she was turned around and wanting to work for him. The strangest part of it is that she even stuck up for him when Sheriff Bowdrie came around trying to kick Brandon and his boys out of town."

"He's still here?" Clint asked.

Nodding as though agreeing to the sky being blue, she said, "Oh yes. Him and all the no-good sons of bitches that he brought with him are all still here. They came in and made themselves at home. There's about eight or nine of—"

She paused when the front door was pushed open so hard that it slammed against the wall. The sound was a jarring bang that echoed throughout the entire cantina. Clint could see some of the folks jumping in their seats, but when they turned to get a look at who'd made the commotion, they quickly turned back around.

Looking back toward the main entrance, Jennifer turned around as well. Her face was slightly pale when she looked at Clint, but her color returned in a second or two. More than that, her cheeks flushed and her eyes took on an angry glint.

"Let me pay for these drinks," she said sternly. "Then we can leave."

Clint took another look at the front door and saw that three men were taking their time walking into the cantina. They weren't particularly big men, but they glared at the rest of the room like tigers picking out the weakest members of a herd. Each of them wore dark suits with waistcoats hanging open to reveal the gun belts strapped around their waists.

"Are those . . . ?" Clint started to ask. But he was cut off by the sharp, insistent tone of Jennifer's voice.

"Let's just go, Clint." Looking up so that she was staring directly into his eyes, she added, "Please."

Even under the best of circumstances, Clint would have had a hard time saying no to those soft lips and those clear hazel eyes. Grudgingly, he got up from his chair and made his way to the bar. He took his time doing so, however, even as the three men in the dark coats walked straight toward him.

Clint could feel Jennifer becoming more tense as she walked behind him. But he still set enough money down on the bar to cover the beers and made sure Paco saw what the coins were for. All the while, the men with the predator's eyes stared at him and showed him blank, unemotional faces.

There were no smug, overconfident grins. All three men glared at Clint with eyes so black they reminded him of looking down three pairs of pistol barrels.

They were the eyes of stone-cold killers.

NINETEEN

"Let me guess," Clint said once he was able to catch up to Jennifer as she moved past him on their way out of the cantina. "Those were Brandon Morris's men."

Since he'd gotten out of the cantina, Clint hadn't seen anything of Jennifer except for her back. She hadn't exactly run out of Paco's, but she was practically gone by the time Clint walked toward the door. He could have either stayed inside and checked up on the men in the dark suits, or he could have caught up with Jennifer.

She didn't seem to care which he picked. In fact, since she'd gotten outside, Jennifer was gaining steam. When she heard Clint's question, however, she stopped and crossed her arms over her chest. Without turning around to face him, she said, "Morris's men? Not hardly."

Clint walked around so he could look her in the face. "Then who are they? Why did you charge out of there so fast?"

"Because there's worse things in town than Brandon Morris or any of the men who work for him."

"Tell me," Clint said. "That's why I'm here with you. That's why I chased you out here when you seemed per-

fectly happy in leaving me in the dust." He could tell that
his words were sinking in, but she wasn't quite over the
chill that had settled over her when those men had walked
through the door. "Come to think of it, why did you leave
me in there? Were you hoping to see me get hurt again?"

The joke might have been tired, but it still had enough
life in it to bring the trace of a smile to her face. "No,"
Jennifer replied. "I left because I knew you'd follow me."

"Well, you got your wish."

"Not quite."

Before Clint could say another word, he felt her hands
press against either side of his face and her lips press
against his mouth. They were every bit as soft as he'd
imagined, and to top it off, she tasted like sweet wine.

The kiss was short, but her mouth lingered on his just
long enough for it to be more than friendly. As she pulled
away from him, she opened her eyes and looked straight
at Clint. From the distance of just a few inches, Clint
couldn't see much more than Jennifer's eyes. The longer
he looked, the more he saw. If it were up to him, he might
not have ever looked away.

"There," she said in a soft voice that seemed so far
from the way she'd sounded before. "Now I got what I
wanted. Well, one of the things anyway."

They were standing outside across the street from
Paco's and the sky was darkening. The wind that rolled
down the street was cool and carried the smell of the
desert. For a couple of moments, Clint and Jennifer were
able to think about nothing but the moment. Unfortunately, the rest of the world had a nasty habit of butting
in right when it wasn't wanted.

Clint was just about to try and extend the moment a
bit longer when he caught a bit of motion out of the corner
of his eye. It came from the front window of the cantina

where a dark figure stepped up to stare outside. Clint recognized the man immediately as one of the well-dressed men with the cold eyes.

Those eyes were still chilling as they glared through the glass at Clint and Jennifer. Since there was no emotion in the eyes or even the face, it was difficult to say which of the two they were specifically looking at. Clint was reminded of the dried-out skulls that could be found on the side of an old trail or half-buried in the desert. Those black sockets were just there, looking out at everything, yet nothing in particular.

Being no stranger to cold, icy stares himself, Clint gave the man in the window one of his own. It was impossible to say whether or not those eyes shifted, but in a matter of seconds, the figure in the window turned and walked farther back into the cantina.

Struggling to put on a friendlier face before looking back at Jennifer, Clint said, "Hospitality sure isn't this town's strong suit."

Jennifer smiled, but only weakly. It wasn't that chilly outside, but she still rubbed her arms as though she'd been standing in a snowstorm. "Those men that came into the cantina," she said, acting as though she hadn't even witnessed the silent exchange that had taken place just moments ago. "They weren't those gunmen I was telling you about before."

"Really? And who might those charmers be?"

"A reminder." She paused to pull in a breath before turning and walking down the street. "They're reminders that no matter how bad things are, they can always get worse."

TWENTY

The man who'd been standing at the window slowly turned until his back was to the glass. The sound of his boots against the floor was like a snake hissing in an empty cave. Everyone at the bar did their best to mind their own business, but they were also too rattled to carry on with their conversations. The result was a sustained, uncomfortable silence.

Ignoring everyone else, the man with the cold eyes stepped up to the bar and placed both hands on top of the polished surface. He stood slightly taller than normal with a solid build that was only accentuated by the cut of his waistcoat. His coat, pants and vest were black as pitch, making the silver watch chain crossing his stomach seem even brighter.

The only spots of skin that could be seen were his neck and face. Even his hands were covered with black leather gloves, which were so clean, it seemed unlikely that they'd touched anything at all in the outside world.

His fingers spread out as he set his hands down, expanding as though he meant to grab hold of the top of the bar and pull it out of the floor.

After what seemed like an unnatural amount of time, the cold-eyed man asked, "Who was that fella who just walked out of here?"

"Fella?" Paco responded, trying to sound ignorant and respectful at the same time. "There's a lot of men that come in and out of here I don't really keep tr—"

The cold-eyed man snapped his hand up and out with such speed that his arm seemed spring-loaded. His fingers took hold of the front of Paco's shirt, but only enough to pull the other man slightly off balance. It wasn't so much a show of force as it was a way to stop the portly bartender from saying another word.

"You know who I mean," the cold-eyed man said. "He was with Jennifer Reid. They were sitting at that table right over there."

Paco looked in the direction that the cold-eyed man was pointing. Sitting at the same table where Clint and Jennifer had been, the other two well-dressed men were now lowering themselves into chairs.

The cold-eyed man tightened his grip slightly and pulled Paco forward just a little bit more. "Now, answer my question. Who was that other man with Jennifer Reid?"

Paco shook his head. "I honestly don't know, Frank. I think I've seen him before, but I don't know where from. Maybe he's one of Jennifer's cousins or something like that."

"She was getting awful friendly with him outside. It didn't look like any way to treat a cousin."

"Then maybe he's an old friend. I just don't know."

Frank narrowed his eyes and stared at the bartender as though he were taking a long, hard look at the fat man's soul. Just as a bead of sweat was starting to push its way out through Paco's forehead, Frank pushed the bartender back and let go of his shirt.

"All right, then," Frank said. "Do me a favor and see if you can find out who that man is. I got a look at him, but I want to make sure my hunch is right. You're the one to do that for me." When he said that last part, Frank pushed the tip of his index finger against Paco's chest. It wasn't a jab, but there was enough strength behind that finger to move the bartender back an inch or so.

Paco nodded quickly. "Sure. I can do that for you." He seemed to sense that he was going to come out of this conversation in one piece. He wasn't quite out of the woods yet, but he was sure eager to get there. "Anything else I can do for you, Frank?"

"Yeah. There is. Bring me a bottle of whiskey and three glasses."

"Sure. No problem."

Without another word, Frank stepped back from the bar and turned to walk toward the table where the other men were waiting. Each of his steps carried weight, but he didn't stomp over the floorboards like many other men did. Where some bigger men would shake the tables as they clomped by, Frank instead made his impression by his very presence.

The other two men waiting at the table were similar in that they were dark figures who sat in their spots, quiet as the grave. Even when Frank sat down in his own seat, none of the three said a word to one another. They didn't make a sound. It was more like three ghouls were haunting the table rather than three men sitting to have a drink.

Like oil spreading over water, the three men's presence caused the tables around them to slowly move aside. People sitting nearby either quietly picked up their glasses

and left or scooted themselves away until they could sit
more comfortably.

Paco rushed over to their table with the bottle and
glasses Frank had requested. Setting one glass down in
front of each man, he opened the bottle and poured some
whiskey before glancing to each man in turn.

"Is there anything else I can get for you?" Paco asked.

None of the men said anything.

"You could . . . ahh . . . just take the bottle and glasses
with you if you were in a hurry to . . . uhh . . . be anywhere."

The biggest of the three men who'd been sitting at the
table turned to look at Paco so slowly that his neck
creaked. A dark beard with gray hairs scattered through
it covered his face. His chin hardly even moved when he
locked eyes with Paco and said, "Leave."

That one word was all the fat man had to hear. Paco
backed up and got out a few mumbled apologies before
hightailing it back behind the relative safety of his bar.
After that, he did his best to pretend that the table and the
three men sitting at it didn't even exist.

One by one, the three men picked up their glasses and
tossed the whiskey down their throats. Not a single one
of them so much as flinched as the alcohol burned through
their systems. Frank reached out to refill his own glass
before handing the bottle over to the bearded man sitting
beside him at the table.

"I got a look at him," Frank said once his glass had
been emptied.

The man with the beard still had a beefy hand wrapped
around the bottle and was preparing to top off his glass
the moment he'd drained the whiskey he'd already
poured. "Yeah?" he said between swigs. "And?"

"It's him."

The third man wore clothes similar to the others, but his coat, vest and pants were dark blue instead of black. He was the smallest of the trio, but rather than look skinny, he seemed sunken and lithe. His face was lean and his eyes were a little too far back into their sockets. "Are you sure?" he asked. "You know Teaghan won't want to hear a word of it unless you're sure."

Frank turned slowly so he could stare directly into the thin man's sunken eyes. "I said it was him, didn't I? What I don't know is how Jennifer Reid knows Clint Adams. I've already got the bartender looking into it and I'll get a few others on the job."

"We could look into it faster ourselves."

"Don't get yourself in a twist," Frank replied. "We all know how to do our jobs. I'll take care of looking into Adams and managing the people who are my eyes and ears. You just do what you're paid to do. Understand?"

The other gunman obviously wasn't used to being spoken to like that, and didn't like it one bit. He nodded grudgingly, however, and refilled his glass with whiskey.

Looking around at each of the other men in turn, Frank tossed back the remainder of his own drink and slowly got up from the table. He didn't have to say anything to the others to know they would do what they were supposed to do. He'd worked with them too long to start doubting them now.

Even after Frank had left, the atmosphere in the cantina was dark and quiet. The other two gunmen left when they were good and ready and even then, the rest of the customers weren't in much of a mood for having fun.

TWENTY-ONE

It felt good to walk. Clint always liked to stretch his legs after a long ride and being in the company of a woman like Jennifer Reid made the experience all the better. She didn't seem ready to go back to her own home either, and led Clint on a casual walking tour of Cielo Grande.

She wasn't pointing out interesting sights, but Clint was taking them in all the same. As far as he could recall, the town was more or less the way he'd left it three years ago. In this part of the country, a town could very well double in size in a year or two. It could also dry up completely, leaving nothing but empty buildings and deserted streets like bleached bones drying in the sun.

The main thing that stuck out in Clint's mind was that burning pile of wreckage that had once been the sheriff's office. Jennifer hadn't explained that just yet, but Clint had the feeling that she was getting around to it. In fact, she hadn't explained a lot of things just yet. Clint didn't mind walking with her and making conversation since he knew that she wanted to tell him the rest of the story in her own time.

Being that it was the start of summer, the daylight hung

on for an exceptionally long time. Clint started to wonder if darkness would ever come since his own internal clock was thrown off a bit from his ride and the overall strangeness of his day.

But, as always, the sun did set and the stars made their presence known over his head. In fact, once dusk had passed, the darkness seemed to overtake Cielo Grande in a rush as though it had been held back too long and was anxious to cover the town. Looking up at the blanket of twinkling gems, Clint let out a low whistle and shook his head.

"What is it about the desert?" he asked. "Even being close to it makes everything seem wider and more open."

Jennifer stood next to him and craned her neck to look upward. A smile formed on her face as well, replacing the troubled expression that she'd been wearing since they'd left the cantina. "Cielo Grande does mean big sky. I guess we're not the first ones to see it, but you're right. It does seem marvelous every time I see all those stars." She took a moment to turn in place and take it all in. "Every time."

Another trait of the desert was the cold that came the moment the sun was gone for the day. It always struck Clint as nature's own way of tipping the balance; a cool, crisp night after a day of blazing hot. Jennifer felt it too and rubbed her arms. It seemed natural, but almost inadvertent for her to step a little closer to Clint until she bumped against his side.

"Sorry," she said, while keeping her body in contact with his.

Clint wrapped an arm around her and replied, "Don't be. I'm sorry to have taken up your day. The time seemed to get away from us."

"It's all right. Business was slow today anyway, and

my sister was looking after the shop. So, does this town seem any different to you now that you're back?"

"Not too much. It does seem a little . . . emptier." Clint had paused before saying that because he'd only put his finger on it just then. It did seem to fit, however, so he let it stay without correcting himself.

Jennifer seemed to agree with his assessment, and nodded slowly. "I always thought I was imagining things, but that seems about right. I've asked folks about that, but they just pretend like everything's just fine. It's probably easier for them that way.

"It sure beats having to admit that you live your life afraid even though you're in your own home. I know plenty of people who've lived here for twenty years, even thirty or forty years. Some of them were born here, but all of them are afraid. They don't admit to it, but you can see it in their eyes. Sometimes I can feel it so much that I want to choke on it."

Jennifer had started walking again. Unlike the way they'd been walking before, she seemed to have chosen a direction and was headed to someplace specific. Her feet smacked hard against the dirt with every step.

Clint had to pick up his own pace to keep up with her. "And here I thought I was helping all those years ago," he told her.

"You were," she said without hesitation. "Believe me, Dutch Dreyman would have killed plenty more people before he was through. Thanks to you, he's a memory."

"Maybe, but it sure seems like everyone's got something else on their minds."

"Isn't that always the way? Once one thing's gone, something always comes along to take its place."

Clint couldn't help but think of all the other people he'd helped out of jams or towns that he'd helped set back on the right path. At the time, he thought he'd been doing the right thing, but now that he saw how Cielo Grande had wound up, a whole other feeling came over him regarding the matter. "Jesus," Clint said. "I hope that's not always the case."

Jennifer looked over at him as if she'd been about to comfort him, but stopped herself before saying anything. She gave him a smile and shrugged. "It probably isn't."

"Tell me the rest of what happened here. I can tell you've wanted to, but there's something holding you back. If you're worried about what I might think, just put that out of your mind. I really want to know."

"I know you do, Clint. That's why I brought you here." She'd come to a stop in front of a small storefront. It resembled a little cabin, but seemed off-kilter mainly because the second floor was only half as big as the one below it.

In the window, there was simple lettering painted directly onto the glass. It read simply, CIELO GRANDE CLOTHIER AND ALTERATIONS. Beneath the sign was a picture of a well-dressed man and woman standing in profile. The design struck Clint as Victorian or even old English.

"This is where I work," Jennifer said. "I also rent the room upstairs."

"Does this mean I have to wait until morning for you to finish what you were telling me?"

"No. It means that we're finally somewhere that I know we can talk without having to worry about being heard. Come on inside and I'll make you some coffee."

Clint followed her into the simple, clean little shop. Like many of the other buildings in town, this one was rickety on the outside, yet done up surprisingly well on the inside. But even in the prim surroundings of the dress shop, Clint couldn't help but feel spooked by the thought of being overheard anywhere in town but this one place.

TWENTY-TWO

Perhaps it was all the dresses and suits hanging from all the different racks, but the main floor of the dress shop seemed to close in on Clint from every side. Everywhere he turned, there was thick material or dark colors blocking his view of a wall or window. The lighter fabrics he did see looked darker or gray at best thanks to the fact that Jennifer was leading him through the place without lighting a lantern.

"Don't worry," she told him as she took his hand and guided him through the almost total darkness. "I know this place like the back of my hand. Besides, there's nothing that you could knock over that would break anyway."

Even so, Clint wasn't accustomed to letting himself be led by the nose. It didn't matter that he was just going through a dress shop; he'd found himself in too many near-fatal situations that started out seeming purely innocent. Instinctively, his guard went up and he was conscious of the weight of the modified Colt hanging at his side.

"Your grip is getting tighter," Jennifer pointed out, referring to the hand that she was holding. "Do you hear someone in here?"

"No," Clint responded. "Just some old habits that are hard to break."

"Well not to worry. Just step carefully because the steps are behind a wall right in front of you. There's a lantern nearby, so try not to break your neck before I get to it."

Clint was about to laugh, but felt his foot knock against a raised threshold, which very well might have caused him to trip if he hadn't been ready for it. Stepping over the raised piece of wood, Clint found himself in a small room that immediately made the hairs on the back of his neck stand on end.

The darkness here was more complete, but he didn't have to see anything to know what was making him nervous. They were standing in a room with walls so close together that it felt like they were in a box. The only thing keeping it from feeling like a coffin was the fact that he had the sense that the room stretched upward a ways.

Soon, he could hear Jennifer handling something made of metal. There was a squeak and then a dim light flared up directly in front of her. She glanced back to check on him before turning the flame on the lantern up just a little more.

"Here we go," she said with a comforting smile. "Almost there."

Clint laughed and motioned for her to carry on. Now that he could see, he felt somewhat awkward for feeling nervous at all. Under normal circumstances, he would have made his way through the shadows without fretting in the least. But with the vision of that blackened pile still in his mind, Clint wasn't really ready to let his guard down.

The stairs were hardly big enough to hold half of Clint's foot. They rose up steeply and were enclosed by a wall that ran all the way up to the top. From where he was standing, Clint could see the room opened up completely at the top of the stairs. The dim glow of starlight filled the room above.

"It's not much," Jennifer said once they'd climbed the staircase. "But it's home."

Clint looked around and noticed the little room was definitely smaller than the shop downstairs, but somehow seemed wide open. There were plenty of windows, none of which were blocked by hanging material or racks of clothes. The bed, which took up most of the room, had a simple wooden frame, but was covered with a thick quilt made of multicolored cotton squares.

There was a vanity on one end of the room and next to it was a wardrobe and dresser. All in all, Clint had been in larger hotel rooms but still felt very comfortable in this little space.

"I hope you don't mind if I keep the light down," Jennifer said as she set the lantern on a small round table beside the bed. "But it's either that or close the curtains and it's such a beautiful night."

"Close the curtains?" Clint asked. "Why would you have to do that?"

She was still smiling as she walked up to the window. Looking out at the stars, Jennifer made sure to maintain some distance between herself and the window. "I . . . I was going to tell you the rest, Clint. I really was. Part of me was thinking that you were the only man who could possibly do anything to make things better around here."

"Well, knowing what the problem is would be a good start."

"I know, but being with you and walking with you has made me feel safer than I've felt in a long time." She shrugged a bit as though she was embarrassed to say what she was saying. "Maybe I've listened to too many of the stories that go around here, but I also know what you did to Dutch Dreyman.

"Nobody else was brave enough to stand up to that asshole, even when he forbid everyone but his own men to wear guns around town. Not even the sheriff bothered to lift a finger." She stepped closer to him, but didn't reach out for Clint until he gently placed his hands on her hands and rubbed her arms soothingly.

It wasn't that she seemed afraid or even vulnerable. Instead, Jennifer just looked like she needed someone to comfort her. When he thought back to the brusque manner she'd had before, Clint figured that she'd held up that facade for so long that she was beginning to buckle under its weight.

Just having his hands on her made Jennifer feel better. She lifted her chin and showed Clint a genuine smile that seemed to sparkle brighter than all the stars combined.

She seemed to be aware of the way she was looking at him and lowered her eyes just a bit. "Do you always do that?"

"Do what?" Clint asked.

"Know exactly what someone needs."

"Yes. Always. And sometimes I grant wishes while I'm at it, but that's only on my really good days."

They both laughed at that and before she could catch herself, Jennifer found herself moving even closer to Clint until she could lay her head on his shoulder. There was a

moment when she stiffened a bit, but Jennifer soon relaxed.

Both of them stayed in that spot for a solid couple of
minutes, enjoying the starlight.

Sharing the dark.

TWENTY-THREE

"You're not going to believe this."

The statement wasn't exactly echoing through an empty room, but it attracted the attention of nearly everyone inside the saloon. The Rusty Spur was one of those places that kept sawdust on the floor because the owner liked it that way. It was the kind of place where the dancers kicked their legs up on stage every bit as much as they did for any man who paid them enough behind closed doors.

The card tables welcomed cheaters and every game played there was as much a sleight-of-hand contest as it was a test of chance and odds. The liquor flowed like water and there was always room for one more at the bar. Even so, the place appeared orderly and even clean. It seemed as though the building and everything in it was unaffected by what went on within the Spur's walls.

Yet despite the fact that the tables were clean and the glasses were polished, it was the kind of place that attracted what upstanding members of society called "a bad element." Some folks had a simpler name for patrons of The Rusty Spur. "Scum" was one of the nicest.

That was also the first word on most decent folks'
minds when they got a look at any one of the people
drinking in the saloon at any particular time. Looking at
them as a whole would probably cause most decent folks
to turn in the other direction and walk away.

Quickly.

The man who'd busted in through the front door of the
saloon and made his announcement had a slender build
and was at least an inch or so shorter than most everyone
else in the place. What he lacked in stature, however, he
more than made up for in attitude.

Wearing a battered bowler that was covered in dust
and worn leathers over a thermal undershirt and beaten
pants, the man put a smile onto his clean-shaven face and
strutted through the saloon as though he owned the place.
Several of the other scum in there offered their greeting
or even a quick wave, but were all ignored.

Instead, the man walked straight to the table at the back
of the room where another man with thick, dusty-brown
hair sat with his feet propped up. A trim little redhead sat
leaning against him wearing a dress that covered just
enough of her so she could be seen in public. The semi-
circle of one pink nipple peeked out from the flimsy material and she didn't so much as try to cover it back up.

Waiting until the man in the bowler got to his table,
the fellow with the redhead beside him asked, "What,
Mike? What aren't I going to believe?"

Mike's face always bore a smile of one kind or another.
Usually, it was a cocky grin meant to get under the skin
of whoever he was talking to. Now, on the other hand, it
was friendlier and even a little excited about what he had
to say.

"You're not going to believe who I saw not too long
ago."

"You just got here and already you're boring the piss outta me," the man seated at the table said. "You're not half as pretty as Allie here, so you better do something to catch my interest."

As if that was her cue, the redhead reached out to slide both hands over the other man's chest. She leaned forward so much that it looked as though she should have fallen out of her chair. But she was practically crawling on him and that was enough to keep her balance. Her small, pert breasts were falling out of her dress even more, which was enough to keep the man's interest.

"I saw Jennifer Reid getting chased out of Paco's."

Hearing that name caused the other man's eyebrows to raise. "That blondie has a nice little body on her, but she's too full of herself."

"Well this'll grab your attention. She was with Clint Adams."

The man seated at the table froze when he heard that. His hand was on the redhead's shoulder, and when he turned to look at Mike, he used it to push the woman back into her own chair. "Are you sure about that?"

Mike nodded. "I was riding with Dutch when he was killed, remember? Hell, I spent some time in prison once old man Bowdrie found his balls and became sheriff. There ain't no way I'm forgetting that face. It's Clint Adams all right. I'd stake my life on it."

A bushy beard covered the face of the man sitting next to the redhead. His fingers went reflexively to his chin whiskers and scratched thoughtfully as he took in what he'd been told. After a moment or two, he looked up to Mike and asked, "What was he doing with that blonde?"

"Not sure. It looked like they were talking about something or other, but I didn't stick around to spy on them."

"Well why the hell not?"

"Because he's seen my face, Brandon. I recognized him, so maybe he'd recognize me. If he did, he'd come after me for sure."

The man at the table was Brandon Morris. Although he was in his mid-thirties, his face seemed younger thanks to a brightness in his eyes. It was that spark that put a lot of people on their guard since he always looked like he was cooking up one thing or another. That spark seemed to flare up even more as he held Mike's gaze.

The whiskers on Brandon's face spread out even further as he grinned from ear to ear. "You think the Gunsmith remembers your sorry face after three years? Maybe he came all this way back here to make sure you were behind bars, since you're this public menace and all."

"Fuck you," Mike said while rolling his eyes. "Excuse me all to hell for thinking you'd want to hear this. I know someone else in town who would appreciate being kept up to speed."

"Aw, don't be such a baby," Brandon said as he swung his feet down from the table and stood up. In two steps, he'd walked around the table and was reaching out to wrap one arm around Mike's neck. Cinching his arm tighter the way one brother would hassle another, he said, "You know you're like my right hand. Even when you cry like a woman, I still couldn't live without ya."

Mike slapped the other man's arm away and tossed a few halfhearted jabs into Brandon's ribs. "Yeah, yeah. Now what are we gonna do about this? I don't mind telling you that having Adams in town makes me nervous."

"I'll just bet it does. Don't think I'm too happy about it either."

"What are we gonna do about it?"

Brandon kept one arm over Mike's shoulder, and led him back toward the back of the room away from the others. "This could be a good thing and I mean good for all of us. We just need to play it right and make sure that we're the ones with all the aces in our hand and not that asshole Teaghan.

"A man like Adams is a wild card. He can make or break the whole game. See what he has to do with that blonde and why he's in town. If he's intending on sticking around here for a spell, find out where he's staying."

"Don't even tell me that all I get to do is spy on him! After what he did to Dutch and putting me in jail I couldn't just—"

"Don't fret about it." Glancing quickly to make sure that nobody was paying them too much attention, Brandon lowered his voice to a whisper. "This could be the end of us or it could be a gift from the Lord almighty. We just can't be stupid about it. Now, I want you to take some of the others with you . . . men that Adams ain't ever seen before . . . and see what he's up to."

"And then what?" Mike asked with growing frustration.

"Then get back to me."

"That's it?"

"For now."

Mike nodded, straightened his hat and started turning back toward the door.

"Hey, Mike." Brandon waited until the smaller man looked over his shoulder at him. "You were right to keep away from Adams. If it comes to us trading shots with him, I'll make sure you get to be the first to pull a trigger. After what he did to Dutch and landing you in prison and all."

That was exactly what Mike wanted to hear and he strode out of the saloon signaling for three other men to follow him along the way.

TWENTY-FOUR

Clint woke up the next morning with Jennifer in his arms. They were both on the bed, fully dressed and on top of the patchwork quilt. Clint had his feet stretched out on the mattress and was leaning against the headboard with Jennifer lying with her head on his leg. His hand was resting on her shoulder, and when he opened his eyes, he thought it was one of the best night's sleep he'd had in a long time.

That was, of course, until he tried to move.

Every muscle in his back and neck screamed for mercy when he tried to stretch. As much as he liked the peaceful look on Jennifer's face, he had to straighten his legs, which shook her out of her own deep sleep. When she stretched her arms, Jennifer still had her eyes closed and her hands moved over the lower part of Clint's body.

Lifting her head, she opened her eyes and smiled. Clint was smiling too, but that was because her hand had wound up resting between his legs.

"Oh," she said with a start. "I didn't mean to . . . I mean I . . ." Jennifer let out an exasperated breath and pulled her hand back. "Good morning, Clint."

He kept the wide smirk on his face mainly because he could tell it embarrassed Jennifer. "Very good indeed."

"Oh stop it," she said while getting up and straightening the front of her dress. As much as she tried to hide it, she couldn't disguise the ruby tint her cheeks had taken. "How did you sleep?"

"Really well," Clint replied, allowing his face to return to normal. "Thanks for letting me stay."

"I know you rented a room, and I didn't mean for you to waste your money, it's just that—"

"Jennifer," Clint interrupted gently. "It's fine. Thank you."

She nodded. "It really was nice having you stay. The least I could do to repay you for keeping me company for so long is to buy you breakfast. Besides, it's easier to talk about things during the morning hours. There aren't so many of them walking about before noon."

Clint decided to keep from asking what she meant by "them" and instead agreed to her offer of breakfast. They left the shop before anyone else came to open the place for business, making Clint feel a bit like a boy sneaking out before a girl's parents caught him with their daughter.

Judging by the way Jennifer hurried out of the shop and straightened everything behind her, she was feeling much the same way.

The sun glared down at them as they stepped outside, reminding Clint just how close he was to miles and miles of desert. It was the dry, arid heat that sucked the moisture from his skin and forced him to cinch his eyelids down to narrow slits.

Since she spent every day in that sun, Jennifer was much more used to it and casually put the edge of her hand to her forehead as though she was batting away the intense beams. She led him down the street to the place where she normally ate breakfast. It was a small room filled with little round tables right next door to a bakery.

Clint had smelled the scent of fresh bread on the air and was glad that she was taking him straight to its source. Even though the place was crowded, Jennifer was recognized immediately and the owners cleared a spot for the both of them to sit.

"We'll have cinnamon biscuits and a pot of coffee," she told the bespectacled man who'd gotten them their seats.

He nodded and hurried off, taking a couple other orders along the way.

Clint wasn't sure if it was the sunlight, the morning air, or the change of scenery, but Jennifer seemed to be back to her old self the moment they'd taken their seats. She'd gotten back some of the fire in her eyes that he'd noticed when they first met. Although it hadn't even been a full day, Clint felt as though he'd seen her emotions come full circle.

"You must think I'm terribly scatterbrained," she said, covering her face with her hand.

"At this point, all you have to do is buy me breakfast and I'll think you're a godsend."

"It's just that things haven't been the same since . . ." she trailed off as she looked around the room. Lowering her voice and leaning toward Clint, she added, "Since the fire."

"I was hoping you'd get back around to that."

"Well, all I wanted to do last night was keep you in one place. I got the feeling that if you heard everything, you might not feel so comfortable spending a quiet night inside."

That made Clint's stomach tighten into a ball. "What do you mean?"

"It means that I know what kind of man you are. I've heard a lot about you, and I've seen what you can do if you have to. You're a man of action," she said with no small amount of admiration in her voice. "We get plenty of liars come through here saying they're some famous bad man, or one of the James boys or a Dalton, but we don't take kindly to the ones who claim to be Clint Adams."

"So do you think I'm really me?"

"Yes." She laughed. "I believe you. I can see it in your eyes." For a moment, she seemed to get lost in Clint's eyes, but quickly shook herself back to the present time and place. "There's no doubt about it."

"Good. Then you should know that I can handle whatever it is you want to tell me. What's more is that I want to know what happened to Sam Bowdrie. I want to know what happened to that building that's lying in a heap down the street and I want to know right now. I think I've waited long enough."

She took a breath, held it for a moment, and then let it out. "You want to know what this is about? You want to know what happened to this town since you've been gone?"

"Yes, I do."

"Well, Brandon Morris came first, but the real damage happened a bit later. It started about a year ago, when a man named Jeremy Teaghan rode in on the five o'clock stage."

TWENTY-FIVE

The front door to the hotel flew open with so much force that it was a small miracle the hinges remained intact. After slamming against the wall with a loud bang, the door was held open by a tall man dressed in a pearl-gray suit with a matching coat. Despite the heat of the sun, the man didn't seem to be the least bit uncomfortable.

He was tall and appeared to be in his late fifties with skin that looked like worn leather. His eyes were squinted and peered out at the world with a smoldering heat that rivaled whatever the summer had to offer. Reaching for the door handle without taking his eyes from the clerk behind the front desk, the tall man stepped inside and closed the door behind him.

The clerk wasn't much shorter than the new arrival, but he cowered like an ant in the shadow of a giant. "G-good mornin' Dave," the clerk stammered. "Is there somethin' I can do for ya?"

Dave walked straight up to the front desk and slammed the palm of his hand down onto the flat wooden surface. He stared down the clerk until the shorter man averted his eyes. Only then did the man in the pearl-gray suit look down at the spot next to where his hand had landed.

The hotel register was lying open on top of the desk and Dave ran one fingertip down each line of signatures until he stopped on the one he'd been looking for. Keeping his finger on that spot like a dagger that had stabbed through the entire register, he turned the book around and lifted his eyes back to catch the clerk's gaze.

"What's this say?" Dave asked.

The clerk looked down, saw the writing and pulled in a breath. He looked up and then down again, obviously reluctant to answer the other man.

Dave reached out with his other hand to take hold of the clerk by the throat. The rest of him didn't move, except for his eyes, which narrowed just a little more. "It's a simple question," he said in a dry, raspy voice. "What does this say?"

The clerk started to say something, but all he could manage was a couple choked syllables. Since the hand around his throat wasn't about to loosen, the clerk sucked in a breath and pushed the words out painfully. "Clint Adams."

Nodding, Dave said, "That's what I thought it said. Now, I thought everyone got the word that if anyone of interest showed up here, Mr. Teaghan was to know about it."

"Th-that's right," the clerk wheezed.

"And don't you think Clint Adams is the interesting sort?"

When he couldn't manage any more words, the clerk nodded. His eyes clenched shut when he realized that nodding was just as painful, only in a slightly different way, as trying to talk.

"So why didn't you come tell us that he was staying in this shit hole of a hotel of yours?" Dave asked. "I can see you're having some trouble talking, so I'll ease up a bit. But if I don't like what I hear, you're gonna wish to God that I just strangled the life out of you right here and now."

True to his word, Dave relaxed his grip. The instant those fingers came away from his windpipe just a little bit, the clerk's face regained some of the color it had lost.

The clerk pulled in a breath and used both hands to grab hold of the counter so he could steady himself before passing out. For a moment, his eyes blinked as though he'd forgotten where he was, but he regained his focus as soon as he caught sight of Dave's weathered face staring straight back at him.

"I didn't have any time," the clerk said quickly. "Mr. Adams just got here and I wasn't able to—"

"It says here that he checked in yesterday," Dave replied in a voice as hard as cold stone. "When I came in here just now, you weren't on your way to tell us, were you?"

The clerk thought about lying, but only for a second. After reconsidering his options, he shook his head as much as Dave's grip would allow.

"Well, at least you were honest," Dave said. "I got to admire any man who's honest. But that still doesn't excuse you for not doing what you're supposed to do. I would have thought everyone in this town would have learned their lesson by now."

The clerk's eyes widened until the whites could be seen all the way around. "We did. I did. I mean, I know what I'm supposed to do."

"Well, it's too late for that. You had your chance to do the right thing, but instead I had to hear about it secondhand and then drag myself all the way down here."

At that moment, the sound of feet beating against the

floorboards rattled through the room from behind the desk. There was a small door leading to private offices that swung open to reveal a pair of lanky boys in their teens. Both of them were wearing gun belts.

"Get away from our pa!" the boy standing in the doorway demanded.

Dave's eyes lingered on the clerk for a moment as his grip tightened around his neck.

Even with the increased pressure around his throat, the clerk rasped, "Boys, get back! Stay out of this!"

The teens stepped into the room, each one taking up position on either side of their father. Rather than try to help loosen Dave's grip, they glared over the desk into the cold eyes of the man in the pearl-gray suit.

His hand hanging over the grip of his gun, the first teen said, "I told you to let go of him."

Dave's eyes flicked one way and then the other, sizing up both of the teens in just under a second. "These your sons?"

Before the clerk had a chance to say another word, Dave's hand snapped away from the register and dropped down to the pistol holstered at his hip. The movement was so fast and so precise that there was no way either of the teens could see it from where they were standing. They did, however, see the glint of steel as it peeked up from over the top of the desk.

Dave pulled the clerk a little to the left and squeezed his trigger. His pistol spat a gout of fiery smoke as lead slapped into the first teen's face. Before that boy could even stagger back from the impact, Dave had pulled the clerk in the other direction so he could get a clear shot at the man's second son.

Even though the shots were echoing through the room and those rock-hard fingers were still locked around his neck, the clerk got out a loud scream. He tried to grab Dave's wrist or even get hold of the gun barrel, but it was too late. The second shot had already been fired and both of the teens were on their way to the floor.

"Every once in a while," Dave said as he pressed the hot end of the gun barrel beneath the clerk's chin, "folks need to have their lessons retaught to them."

Tears were streaming down the clerk's face, and his hands flailed helplessly against the desk as well as the front of Dave's chest.

"Since you weren't good for shit in doing what you were told," Dave continued. "I guess you can do some good in giving this town a refresher course in what they need to do to keep Mr. Teaghan happy."

Turning to the crowd he knew would be gathering outside the hotel's front window, Dave squeezed the clerk's throat a little tighter and pulled the sobbing man off his feet and over the desk. He forced the clerk to look toward the window before pressing his gun's barrel to the back of his head.

"Don't fear God or the devil," Dave shouted to anyone within earshot. "Fear Jeremy Teaghan."

Dave pulled his trigger, sending most of the contents of the clerk's skull outward to splatter onto the wall and window. The bullet shattered the plate glass as it flew out through the man's forehead.

TWENTY-SIX

Clint's attention was pulled away from what Jennifer had been saying when he heard screams coming from outside the restaurant. Without hesitation, Clint jumped up from his seat and rushed over to the front door. Jennifer was right behind him.

Looking in the direction he'd heard the scream, Clint spotted a group of people converging a ways down the street. They seemed to want to form a group, but were having trouble staying together and kept breaking apart like a poorly made piece of machinery.

Although he could hear anxious voices, Clint was having a hard time catching any words as he made his way toward the loose gathering. Every one of his senses were on the lookout for any sign of trouble. All he caught, however, was more distressed voices and another round of panicked screams.

The woman making the loudest noise was an older lady with streaks of gray running through her black hair. She was taller than most of the folks around her and stood out because she wore a dress that looked more suited for winter than the heat of summer. The dark purple and black material swirled around her as she dashed from one person to another trying to get someone to pay her some attention.

"What's the matter with you people?" she screamed. "Didn't any of you see what happened to my husband? Are you all blind?!"

Clint quickened his pace so he could get to her. Before he got close enough to catch her eye, another figure stepped in front of him and was nearly knocked over as Clint slammed directly into him.

"Back up!" said a man who was shorter and had a head covered with sweat and stubble. "Keep movin' before I . . ." The rest of what he was about to say tapered off once he got a look at who he was speaking to. Suddenly, his eyes widened and he shouted, "Mike! Get your ass over here!"

"What happened?" Clint asked.

The shorter man reached out and put his hand flat against Clint's chest, holding him at arm's length. "Never mind that. All you need to know is that you should come with me."

Although the woman had stopped screaming, she was glancing nervously between Clint and the man who was holding him back. In fact, everyone nearby had quieted themselves and some were even slinking away as if trying not to be noticed.

"Get out of my way," Clint demanded. By this time, he'd seen enough panic in people's eyes to know there was something very bad going on. "I want to know what happened here."

"Never mind that. Just come with me before something else happens." With that, the smaller man made a big mistake. His hand dropped down to the gun at his side and took hold of the pistol's grip. Even though he didn't pull the gun from its holster, he'd done more than enough to justify what happened next.

Clint reached out and closed his hand over the other man's, keeping both palms over the gun and the weapon lodged firmly in its holster. Taking one step forward so one of his legs was positioned behind the other man's shins, he used his free hand to sweep up and over until his forearm connected with the shorter man's chest.

Without use of both hands to balance himself, the shorter man staggered back the moment Clint's arm connected with his torso. That impact pushed him back even farther until his heels met up with the leg Clint had already positioned. From there, it was a matter of too much momentum and too little balance and the shorter man toppled straight back to land with a rush of air spewing from his lungs.

After a quick look to make sure the other man was down for the moment, Clint stepped over him and continued walking toward what he thought was the source of the commotion. The woman in the black and purple dress was wringing her hands nervously, but seemed rooted to her spot.

"Ma'am," Clint said, making his way to the distressed older woman. "What's the m—"

His question was cut off by a sharp left jab, which Clint had no way of seeing before it reached his jaw. The punch was thrown from behind a confused local man who hadn't moved fast enough to reveal the other man who'd been coming up behind him.

Clint's head snapped to one side, rolling with the unexpected punch as best he could. When he brought his eyes back around, he was looking straight into the youthful face of the one who'd been called over by the guy still trying to get to his feet.

Mike smirked as he snapped out another punch. This time, however, Clint was ready for it.

TWENTY-SEVEN

A man in a pearl-gray suit walked into Clint's field of vision, but remained beyond the group of locals. He stood with his shoulders squared and his hand hovering near his holstered pistol. After watching for less than a second, he turned and kept walking down the street. That man was also much farther away than the one taking a swing at him, so Clint was forced to turn his attention elsewhere.

While he'd been watching the man in the gray suit and matching coat, Clint had felt his reflexes kick in to respond to the punch being thrown his way. His hand snapped upward with fingers outstretched, just in time to intercept Mike's fist.

Knuckles slapped against Clint's palm with a loud crack and Clint made a fist before Mike could retract his arm. The smug grin that had been on Mike's face only moments before was replaced by a frustrated grimace. Soon, that disappeared as well, to be replaced by a painful groan as Clint's fist drove into his gut.

Before Mike keeled over completely, Clint sent another straight punch into his temple. He knew that would rattle Mike's brain for a little bit, so Clint let go of the fist he'd caught and swung around to face the skinny man who was just climbing back to his feet.

"This doesn't have to be so hard," Clint said as he prepared for whatever might be coming his way next. "If you fellas would learn how to answer a man's question, you might find yourself not getting knocked around so damn much."

The skinny man with the face full of stubble looked first at Clint and then over to Mike. He looked like a dog that wasn't used to doing anything without hearing the proper command first.

In response to the skinny guy's confused expression, Mike shouted, "Knock him on his ass, Stick!"

Clint smirked and moved forward the instant he saw the resolve in the skinny man's eyes. "You go by Stick, huh? That's appropriate."

With that, Clint faked a punch to the other man's chin and waited for the response. Sure enough, Stick lifted both arms to block the blow that never came, leaving himself wide open for Clint's fist which drove deep into his stomach and doubled him over.

Rather than hit him again, Clint took hold of Stick by the back of his shirt collar as well as his belt and tossed him headfirst into the wet ground in front of the nearest water trough. He landed with his face in the grime and sank an inch or two with a wet, sucking sound.

"Every time I hear someone mention a stick in the mud," Clint said, "I'll think of you."

Stick didn't take kindly to that at all. He picked himself up and swiped at some of the bigger chunks of mud that hung from him and his clothes. Getting himself upright, he started to reach for the gun at his side, but paused when he saw Clint looking sternly back at him.

Although Clint still had the remnants of a smile on his

face, he let his eyes reflect the fact that he was still ready to do business if the need arose. His hand didn't move, but stayed relatively close to the modified Colt hanging at his side. That, and a warning shake of his head was enough to make Stick back down and accept his place in the mud for the time being.

The sound of steel brushing against leather was quiet, yet unmistakable. Like a knife being drawn from its scabbard, it flowed through the air and seemed loud as cannon fire to the ears that were listening for it.

Of course, Clint had been listening for it.

He figured Mike would go for his gun sooner or later and hearing that sound only told him he'd been right. Turning around in one fluid motion, Clint made himself ready to draw, but kept himself from doing so. Something in his gut told him that things weren't about to go that far awry.

Looking at Clint with a warning stare of his own, Mike aimed his pistol at him and kept the weapon at hip level. "Look here, now. I didn't come out here to shoot you, but I will if'n I don't have any other choice."

"I was just about to say the same thing," Clint said. His body was more relaxed now that he'd had a chance to size up both other men. There was no doubt in Clint's mind that he could draw and fire before he was in any real danger himself.

Mike's features were tense, but controlled despite the nasty discoloration that took over the part of his face Clint had punched. A dark knot was already swelling up there as well. "Besides, you're Clint Adams, right?"

"Last time I checked."

"Then that means you're the type that listens to reason."

Clint had to laugh at that. "Where I come from, listening to reason doesn't usually involve knocking each other senseless. What about you?"

Nodding, Mike lowered his gun and slid it back into its holster. "How's that? Better?"

"Much. Now what was going on here? Who was screaming?"

"Never mind that. Just come along with me."

Clint shook his head once more. The sound of someone sloshing in the mud came back to his ears, so he snapped his fingers and shot a mean look over toward Stick.

The skinny man stopped where he was and looked over at Mike. Since he didn't get much of anything from him either, Stick spat out a curse and let himself drop back down into the grime.

Smirking at the other man's frustration, Clint said, "I'm not going anywhere until I talk to someone in charge."

"How about Brandon Morris?" Mike asked. "Will he do?"

After thinking it over for a moment, Clint nodded. "Sure."

"And what about Stick?" Mike asked. "You mind if he tags along?"

"Just tell him to keep his distance. I'd rather not get that filth all over my clothes."

Mike nodded over to where Stick was waiting before turning and walking off down the street. The crowd had dispersed by this point and only a few small groups of locals watched what was going on from the boardwalk and storefronts.

Making sure both the other men were where he could see them, Clint fell into step behind them.

TWENTY-EIGHT

The Rusty Spur caught Clint's eye the moment he, Mike and Stick rounded the corner. The place wasn't very big, but the sign looked a little out of place since it was nailed to a tidy little storefront that could very well have been the home of a sewing circle. It struck Clint just then that he was used to saloons being big and noisy and every bit as unkempt as the men who usually ran them. But The Rusty Spur was none of those things.

Well, not as far as he could see, anyway.

"That's the place," Mike said, pointing to the little saloon.

Clint nodded in that direction. "I was meaning to check in on that place, but I've been a little busy since I got into town."

"Yeah. I'll bet you have."

That was pretty much the extent of the conversation among the three men. Other than that small exchange of syllables, the trio walked without a sound into the saloon. There were a few others around, but they made a path for them the instant they saw Mike and Stick headed toward them. When they saw Clint's face, the locals gazed on as if they'd just spotted a ghost.

The inside of the place was just what Clint would have expected after seeing the outside. Clean tables and an orderly bar with bottles lined up in tidy rows behind it. Even the mirror was kept polished to an impressive shine and the dust on the floor seemed to have been freshly laid down. Turning his attention from the things inside the saloon to the people around him, Clint picked out the man they were probably there to see without much trouble at all.

He was the man sitting at one of the back tables who didn't look away from or particularly impressed by the group of three men walking through the saloon. It was the other man's beard that tipped Clint off, however. Despite it being bushy and sprawling over the man's entire face, every whisker was in place and the whole beard looked tidy and well managed.

Sure enough, the man with the beard stood up just as Mike and Stick brought Clint over to his table. "Well I'll be damned, if it ain't Clint Adams in the flesh," he said, extending a manicured hand. "The name's Brandon Morris."

Clint nodded and shook Brandon's hand. "Nice place you've got here."

The other man looked around proudly. "Most men don't take pride in what they do anymore. I like to do things the right way, whether it's running my saloon or just tending to my own personal affairs."

Deciding to test Brandon right away, Clint asked, "So which of your personal affairs got you run out of El Paso?"

Although a shadow rolled over Brandon's face, he didn't let the wave of anger show any more than that.

Instead, he swallowed it down and nodded as if he'd just lost a game of cards. "That's a fair question, Adams. Although a bit rude considering I was about to buy you a drink."

"Were you?" Clint asked innocently. "Then I'll apologize once I get my drink. I'll take a beer."

The smile on Brandon's face seemed completely genuine as he glanced over to the bartender and snapped his fingers. "Two beers." After that, he dropped himself down into his chair and kicked out the empty chair directly across the table from him. "Take a load off, Adams," he said, pointing to the chair, which was still rocking.

Clint picked up the chair by its back and scooted it around so that not too much of the room was to his back. As he sat down, the bartender was walking over with two full mugs of beer in his hands.

"I suppose this is when you tell me to get the hell out of your town," Clint said. "Or were you going to start by threatening me like the two you sent out after me?"

"Who threatened you?" Brandon asked. When he saw the guilty look on Mike's face, he shook his head and sipped his beer. "Then I guess I owe you an apology too, Adams. They were supposed to ask real nicely for you to join me. How about we call it even?"

"I can live with that," Clint said as he lifted his mug and took a sip for himself.

The beer was clean and did wonders to wash away the gritty taste that was still lingering in the back of Clint's throat. After he'd set his mug down and saw that Brandon had done the same, Clint looked around and noticed that there were no gunmen standing nearby.

"I see you called your men off," Clint pointed out.

Brandon shrugged. "First of all, there's nobody lookin' for trouble in here. Second, even if you did want trouble, there's not a lot me or my men could do about it."

Although he didn't confirm the other man's take on the situation, Clint didn't try to deny it either. "So your men weren't out starting trouble when I happened to cross paths with them?"

"No. Why?"

Suddenly, Clint felt his stomach twist. "Because there was someone screaming not too far from where they were."

Hearing that, Mike leaned in on the table as if from out of nowhere. "I was gonna tell you that, Brandon. There was a shooting down on Mesa Street."

Clint was out of his seat and stepping back from the table the instant he heard that. "Mesa Street? My hotel's on Mesa Street."

Brandon's eyes grew wide, and he pushed away from the table as well. "I'm not a firm believer in coincidences, Adams. My guess is this has something to do with what I wanted to talk to you about. Why don't I come with you and talk it over along the way?"

Clint felt as if he'd wasted enough time already. Thinking that he'd found the source of the screams when he'd stumbled on the two who'd attacked him, Clint turned and strode from The Rusty Spur in a way that told everyone around him that he wasn't about to be stopped. Brandon hurried to catch up and they both left the saloon in a quick stride.

As he rushed down the street, Clint heard a muffled laugh coming from the man keeping pace with him. "What's so funny?" he asked.

Brandon shook his head, his breath starting to come in puffs as he ran. "You, Adams. I wonder if you stir up this much trouble in every damn town you go to."

"I wonder that same thing sometimes, myself."

TWENTY-NINE

It didn't take much of a detective to follow the troubled faces and panicked locals back to the Casa Verde Hotel. Part of what made it so easy for Clint was that there weren't so many locals milling about obscuring his view. Also, a part of him figured that if it was trouble, it was probably somehow connected to him. For most people, that would have been a self-centered way to look at the world.

Unfortunately, Clint wasn't like most people in that respect.

The front window of the hotel was broken and the shards of glass that remained in the frame were covered with blood and worse. Through the window, Clint could see a few others standing looking down at something. When he got closer, he could see the bodies lying in a row on the dirty floor.

A woman in a black and purple dress ran toward Clint waving her finger. "You! You bring this on us! What's wrong with men like you who kill and kill and are never happy with the blood you spill?"

Someone came from the others who were standing

nearby to quiet the woman, but her words still echoed in Clint's ears. Was that why he'd been getting so many strange looks while he was in town? Did people think that about him wherever he went and was recognized? Rather than let himself be bogged down by questions he couldn't answer, Clint stepped forward to see what he could do.

He recognized the clerk's face the instant he saw it. The features were obscured by blood and blackened by smoke, but that was definitely the same man who'd checked him into the hotel the night before. Brandon stepped up beside him and took in the carnage with a low whistle.

"Jesus Christ almighty," Brandon said.

Clint spun around and took hold of Brandon's shirt-front using both fists. Nearly pulling him off his feet, Clint twisted the other man around and spoke directly into his face.

"What the hell is wrong with you?" Clint snarled, his temper flaring. "There's three men dead here, and you look like you're taking in a floor show."

"What would you have me do? Bring 'em back to life? I can't do that any more than you can."

"Then why are you so goddamn smug?"

"Because now you get a look at what it's been like in Cielo Grande since you left. Now you get to see what folks here have to live with every day."

"When I left, there were three less killers in the world and a good man about to put on a badge. What else was I supposed to do? I'm no miracle worker either, you know!"

Brandon didn't say anything just then. He also didn't struggle to get out of Clint's grasp, either. Instead, he looked from one side to the other, drawing Clint's attention in that direction as well.

Although he wasn't about to let go of Brandon just yet, Clint looked where he was being directed and saw several shocked faces staring back at him. The people gathered around weren't particularly threatening and most of them weren't even armed. They did share one common bond, however, besides the fact that they all hailed from the same town.

They were all scared. Too scared, in fact, to do anything else but watch and wait to see what else was going to happen.

Still not letting go of Brandon, Clint turned to the closest person he could see. "Did you see who did this?" he asked.

The local's eyes widened before he started nodding.

Clint held Brandon toward the other man and asked, "You know who this is?"

The local nodded without hesitation.

"Was it one of his men?"

The local shook his head.

"Are you sure?"

Again, without hesitation, came the nod.

Seeing that, Clint let go of Brandon, turned away from the three corpses and walked outside. Once he was outside, Clint didn't have to look hard to find a spot where he was away from prying eyes. It seemed the locals couldn't get away from him fast enough.

Clint watched Brandon come out of the hotel. One thing he was surprised to see was that many of the locals didn't shy away from the man with the bushy beard. In fact, Brandon took a moment to ask a few questions and got his answers relatively quickly.

"Let me guess," Clint said once Brandon had walked up to him. "It was one of Teaghan's men who did this."

Brandon nodded. "Just one of them, but one of the

worst. Just one day in town and you already got a good feel for the lay of the land, huh?"

"Yeah. I'm also getting the feeling I'm overstaying my welcome."

Brandon looked confused for a second, but all it took was a quick look over his shoulder to clear that up. "Don't worry about them. They're just scared. That's how Teaghan operates. He's a cold-blooded bastard, but all he needs to do is send a message every now and then to get some breathing room."

"This was a message?" Clint asked.

"Yep. He's not exactly the type to write letters."

Clint shook his head while watching the locals go about the nasty business of cleaning up their dead.

"This is what I wanted to talk to you about, Adams," Brandon said, cutting in on Clint's thoughts. "Whatever business you may have with me, I'll be more than happy to deal with it. If you were just passing through and didn't know my name from Adam, then I guess you coming here is even more . . . what's the word . . ." After searching his brain for a moment or two, Brandon's face lit up like the Fourth of July. "Fortuitous! That's the word."

"Seems like everyone wants to talk to me, but they don't say much once I let them," Clint said. "Since I've just decided to take up some business with Jeremy Teaghan, I'll listen to you while I walk."

"Fine with me. I'll even lead the way."

Clint looked over at the man who was supposed to be one of the baddest men in town. So far, Brandon Morris seemed like he had the potential to do wrong, but genuinely shared some of Clint's own concerns. Sometimes, things just worked out like that.

"Start talking," Clint said as he and Brandon both started walking.

THIRTY

"Look there," Brandon said, pointing off to the right as they rounded the corner that took them off of Mesa Street.

Clint had already been looking in that direction even before he'd been asked to. That was the location that had marked where his visit to Cielo Grande had been run off into a ditch. It was the heap of burned rubble and ash that had once been the town sheriff's office.

Looking over there himself, Brandon said, "That there is the biggest message left by our mutual friend Jeremy Teaghan. I'd been in town awhile and was just starting to sink some roots."

Clint smirked without the first trace of humor. "Roots? From what I've heard, your kind of roots aren't exactly the kind this town needed."

"Eh, it was small-time stuff really. I made my face known and laid some groundwork, but didn't hurt anyone along the way. Mainly I wanted to set up a reputation for myself so I could live here without worrying about the sheriff. Old man Bowdrie was a hell-raiser, that's for damn sure."

Strangely enough, Clint detected an odd sort of admiration in Brandon's voice when he talked about the ex-sheriff.

"He locked away plenty of my friends, but not without good reason," Brandon continued. "A man in my line of work knows the risks and only the stupid ones are too quick to draw a pistol when they could get a lot further by spending a few dollars or bending a few ears in the right direction."

The more time he spent with Brandon Morris, the more Clint remembered about the man. He'd heard of him from some acquaintances in El Paso as well as from a few lawmen from that part of the country. Although there were plenty of stories about Brandon being a royal pain in the ass, the warrants out for him were mostly of the thieving sort. As far as Clint could recall, Brandon wasn't even known to be a very good shot.

Looking over at Brandon, Clint said, "It sounds like you should have gone into business, then. Wouldn't that have been better than threatening people and taking on a small town's sheriff?"

"That's just it. I never took on Sheriff Bowdrie. It was easier and better all around for me to avoid the old man. Sure, we butted heads a bit, but it wasn't nothing serious. Actually, we almost had a nice little arrangement until Jeremy Teaghan came to blow everything to hell."

They'd rounded the corner and turned onto Military Avenue. From what Jennifer had told him, they were still headed in the right direction to find where Teaghan hung his hat. Even with the charred remains out of sight, Clint could still smell the hint of ash lingering in every breath he took.

"Let me guess," Clint said. "He started with the sher-iff."

"No. Actually, he started with me. We had a few scuf-

fles here and there, but I was on the losing end of most
of 'em. There were one or two that I can remember where
I came out on top, but that was due to some . . . well, let's
say . . . creative planning on my part.

"The men he hired were just too much for me to handle, so I backed off. I bought my saloon and ran what
little business I could without drawing too much attention."

"You could have left town," Clint pointed out.

"A man like me can't afford to pick up and leave too
often. We get seen as weak. Plus, I'm stubborn and wasn't
about to give Teaghan the satisfaction. I also thought I
could stick around and wait for my chance to move him
out. Anyhow, that's when Teaghan started in on the next
pain in his ass—our esteemed Sheriff Bowdrie.

"Ol' Sam was content to let me and Teaghan fight
among ourselves just so long as no innocents got in the
cross fire. He gave us both a hard time, but made sure we
knew not to hurt anyone not involved with our disputes."

While it wasn't the most accepted way of doing things,
it sounded as though Bowdrie was enforcing what laws
he could with the limited manpower at his disposal. Once
again, Clint had to admire the old man for both of those
things.

"Once he figured I was out of his way," Brandon went
on to say, "Teaghan started staking his claim to this whole
town. He started by muscling in on every business and
laying the groundwork to become the boss of the whole
place."

"Why here?" Clint asked to himself as well as to the
man walking beside him. "Why Cielo Grande?"

"Why not? This town's the last stop for a hell of a lot
of miles before hitting the desert. It does its fair share of
business. But, speaking as a man who understands how

someone like Teaghan thinks, the only real reason to control a place like this is because he can."

"You're right," Clint said. After all, he'd seen power-hungry types all too many times himself. They lived to devour whatever they could and nothing else. They were greedy for the sake of being greedy. Simple minds, yet still difficult for someone like Clint to fully understand.

He understood those men the way most folks understood a clock. They knew how the hands were supposed to move and which way they turned, but were still strangers to the true inner workings. What it all boiled down to was that Clint really didn't want to know how such men's minds worked.

There was already plenty of ugliness to see in the world.

"I know I'm right," Brandon replied. "If I had the power, I might have done the same thing as Teaghan." After saying that, Brandon actually stopped where he was and cocked his head to one side. "Naw. Forget that. I'd probably be doing the same thing I am now, only a little more lucrative if I had my say. The outlaw trail hasn't really worked out for me. Maybe I just don't have what it takes. Now, Jeremy Teaghan's got what it takes. The proof is right back in that pile of dirt back there."

"Tell me about it."

"Simple story really. Sam Bowdrie started in on Teaghan and wouldn't let up. Teaghan tried to bribe him and Sam spit on the money and arrested the men who delivered it. Teaghan tried to threaten him and Sam ignored it and ran down the men sent to give him a hard time.

"What separates men like me from men like Teaghan is how far they're willing to go." For the first time since he'd started talking, Brandon seemed to lose his casual demeanor. His face even paled a bit before he started talking again. "Teaghan doesn't show his face much, but he paid a personal visit to Sheriff Bowdrie one night. He made sure the whole town was there to watch, too.

"He called out the sheriff and Sam came out with all his deputies. All three of them."

"Three?" Clint asked. "That's all he had?"

Brandon nodded. "The rest were scared away or fired by Sam himself for taking bribes or such. Anyway, a dozen men wouldn't have done any good that night. Once Sam made it clear that he wasn't going to let up until Teaghan either left town or cleaned up his ways, that was pretty much the end of him."

"Yes, Mr. Morris," came a voice that took both Brandon and Clint by surprise. "It most certainly was."

Clint's eyes snapped up and toward the source of the voice. His hand had reflexively dropped over his gun, but he paused before clearing leather.

The man who'd interrupted Brandon's story was standing in front of an unmarked storefront in the middle of the block. Flanked on both sides by tall men with cold eyes, wearing dark, finely tailored suits, was a man in his early forties wearing a dark suit of his own.

Clint didn't have to be told who that man was. The well-dressed figure matched all the descriptions he'd heard and was standing at the address Jennifer had given him.

"Jeremy Teaghan," the man said. "At your service."

THIRTY-ONE

Clint looked at each of the well-dressed men in turn. Despite the fact that he'd come so close to drawing his own gun, none of the men in front of them had so much as batted an eye. That either meant they didn't know how close Clint had been to drawing or they didn't care.

Judging by the cool alertness in those men's eyes, it was obvious to Clint that they knew damn well what was going on. Those men were just not the types to be rattled by much of anything.

Teaghan stepped forward. He was about the same height as Brandon, but with a clean-shaven face and long, thick hair, which reached down to his shoulders. That hair came down to cover a good portion of his forehead, too, but still appeared to be tended and well cared for. A patch covered his left eye, but the eye that remained burned with enough intensity to make up the difference.

"You were just getting to the best part," Teaghan said as he stepped down off the boardwalk and onto the street. "Please continue."

Even though Brandon was smiling, there was no mistaking the fact that he was uncomfortable being where he was. Despite that, however, he did his best to maintain his composure and look relaxed when he replied, "I wouldn't dream of it. Telling this part seems to be one of your favorite hobbies."

"So true," Teaghan said. "I do find it helps for me to say it myself." Turning to Clint, he said, "I trust Mr. Morris has told you everything leading up to my visit with the sheriff? Anyhow, the important thing for you to know is that Mr. Bowdrie was incapable of listening to reason. I know he was a friend of yours, Mr. Adams, but he wasn't the smartest of men."

"I didn't know Sam Bowdrie as well as I would have liked," Clint responded. "But he struck me as a good man who would make a fine sheriff."

"Perhaps, but he was by no means a smart man." Teaghan's eyes narrowed since he could tell that his words were ruffling Clint's feathers. Although he didn't seem to mind the disturbance he caused, Teaghan waited another moment to see if Clint was going to do anything about it. He smiled arrogantly when he saw that he could continue.

"This town doesn't need a mayor," Teaghan announced. "And it doesn't need a sheriff. All it needs is someone to manage its business and handle its finances. That someone is me.

"My men gunned down the deputies without a problem. If I remember correctly, a few of the townspeople even tried to lend a hand. Is that right?"

Since Teaghan seemed to be looking to Brandon for an answer to that question, Clint looked over to him as well. Brandon made an effort to keep from saying what he wanted and instead nodded once to verify what had been said.

"Now I remember," Teaghan said. "A good number of

them tried to help, but they had to be eliminated as well. But even though those misguided locals had to be killed outright, I made sure the deputies were merely incapacitated." Locking eyes with Clint, Teaghan added, "Shot through the kneecaps. Very nasty."

Rarely had Clint ever seen a man like Teaghan. Every bone in his body told Clint that Teaghan was telling what had truly happened. The amazing part was that Teaghan didn't seem the least bit remorseful about any of it. In fact, he seemed to take true joy in every gruesome detail.

"Your sheriff friend was shot through the stomach," Teaghan went on to say. "I'm sure you know, Mr. Adams, that it takes a while to die from wounds like that. After all, I had to make sure they would live to fully experience the flames once I set that office to the torch.

"I can still hear the screams," Teaghan said as though he was fondly remembering a particular summer day from his youth. "The smell of skin cooking was a bit like beef roasting over a fire except a bit . . . gamier. The message was simple, Mr. Adams. I am not the law here, but to these people I am God and the devil. My word is to be obeyed; otherwise the penalty is death."

Teaghan was standing in the street by this time, no more than four or five paces in front of Clint and Brandon. The other men in suits were in their same places. Each of them had their hands on their guns, and each of them had their eyes on Clint.

"Three men already died because of you, Mr. Adams," Teaghan announced. "I'm sure you've already seen their bodies at your hotel. Be a good chap and leave my town. I'll give you until the morning, so you can rest up and prepare for your trip. If you're here tomorrow, I'll have you gunned down as well as anyone else who tries to help you or even looks at you in a way I don't like.

"This is my town, Mr. Adams. You had your chance to protect it, but now it's time for you to step aside. Heed my words and if you can't remember the penalty for ignoring them, just ask your friend Sam Bowdrie."

THIRTY-TWO

Every muscle in Clint's body tensed.

Every piece of him wanted nothing more than to draw his Colt and start drilling holes into Jeremy Teaghan. From there, he could pick off Teaghan's men one by one until there was nothing left but an empty street, smoke in the air and a whole lot of blood on the ground.

Clint wanted these things so badly he could taste them, but didn't make a move to see those desires through. Mainly, he held back because Teaghan and his men were all waiting for Clint to lose his temper and tip his hand.

No good ever came from fighting out of anger. Emotion had its place, but as fuel to the fire, not a man's single driving force. Besides all that, Clint needed to do something else besides simply draw and shoot. He'd tried that once already and it hadn't worked out too well.

"All right, then," Clint said while nodding and taking a step back. "Have it your way. I've had enough of listening to all this hot wind anyhow."

And with that, Clint stepped away from the storefront where Teaghan was standing like an emperor and left. He kept his ears open for the first sound of someone making a move.

There was silence as Teaghan waited for a response. The only sound that came back to him was the dry crunch of Clint's boots against the ground. Brandon looked over to Teaghan, shrugged and then headed off after Clint himself.

Teaghan took one step forward and lowered his hand to his gun. His face began to fill with a rage that didn't seem to fit upon his features. The calm facade that was so much a part of him cracked, and he almost resorted to drawing his weapon out of sheer frustration.

"Don't walk away from me, Adams!" Teaghan shouted. "Nobody ignores me. You understand? Nobody!" The more he shouted, the more Teaghan's voice lost its civility and deteriorated into something much more brutish. "Them that ignores me get hurt! Remember that and don't forget to get your fucking ass out of my town!"

Clint's mind filled with plenty of things he wanted to say, but he kept himself in check. His muscles twitched to do one of a dozen things to resolve the situation, but still he kept himself in check and kept walking a straight line down the street away from the storefront.

Teaghan was still shouting, but Clint had already gotten himself to block out the other man's voice completely. There must have been some pretty foul language, because Brandon was cringing when he finally caught up and walked next to Clint.

"Well, if you weren't thinking of leaving before, you might want to start now," Brandon said. "I've never seen Teaghan that angry."

"Good," Clint replied. "Let him rant. I've got better

things to do than listen to him squawk and watch him strut."

"Better things, huh? Like watching over your shoulder?"

"No. Like doing what I should have done the last time I was here."

THIRTY-THREE

"Oh, my god," Jennifer said as she dropped what she was doing and rushed over to Clint. "Where have you been?"

Having left her high and dry at the restaurant where they'd had breakfast, Clint hoped that Jennifer would know better than to try and follow him once he got into the scuffle with Brandon's men. After seeing that she would let him take care of his business alone, Clint figured that Jennifer would do the right thing and not get herself too involved.

Safe or not, she didn't look at all happy.

Clint had barely gotten a chance to step into the dress shop before he was spotted. He'd seen Jennifer through the front window and was mighty glad to have found her after only looking in one other place.

Kneeling in front of a young girl who was standing on a short-wooden stool modeling a pink dress with both arms held straight out to her sides, Jennifer looked over at Clint with wide, worried eyes. She'd been completing an alteration to the girl's dress, and when she'd seen Clint step inside the shop, she let the needle drop from her hand. It dangled from the end of a white thread and swung almost low enough to scrape the floor.

"I don't know if I should hug you or slap you," she said. "After seeing you get into a fight with those men and then just leaving like that, I think I'd be justified either way."

"I didn't just leave you. I knew you'd—"

"You sure did just leave me! With everything going on, anything could have happened to you."

"All right then, out of those two choices you gave me, I'll take the first one."

Even though she'd been the one to say it, it took Jennifer a moment to realize what Clint was talking about. She soon shook her head, walked up closer to him and gave him a hug. Once her arms were around him, she let out the breath she'd been holding and squeezed him tighter.

"It hasn't been that long, but there's still plenty of talk going around about you," she said. "First, I heard that you were over at The Rusty Spur talking to Brandon Morris, and then I hear you were facing off with Jeremy Teaghan."

"Now that's a switch," Clint said with amusement. "For once, everything you heard about me was completely true."

She looked at him as though she didn't believe him. Then, once she saw he was serious, she looked as if she didn't want to believe him. "You talked to both of them? Already?"

"And why wouldn't I?" Clint asked, stepping back and holding his arms outstretched. "I am the big legend, aren't I?"

Even the little girl standing with the needle hanging from her dress had to snicker at that. Jennifer wasn't so quick to give in, but even as she crossed her arms and looked back at him, she couldn't keep the smile from creeping onto her face.

"I'm still mad at you," she told him. "I was worried sick. It was all I could do to just come here and hope you had the sense to find me."

"Actually, I was hoping to talk to you. Do you have a minute?"

"Oh, go on," came a voice from behind Jennifer. It belonged to an older woman whose long, braided hair was more gray than light brown. She was already kneeling in front of the little girl and picking up the needle that Jennifer had dropped. "I'll finish up with Megan here."

Jennifer spun around and asked, "Are you sure? Clint's survived this long. He can wait until my work's done here."

"After all the fretting you've done about him today, I doubt you'll be any use to me now," the older woman said. "Go on, but don't forget about that bridal gown for Virginia Tuppen. It needs to be done by the end of the week."

"I haven't forgotten. Thank you so much." Jennifer wrapped her arms around the older woman, being careful to embrace her around the shoulders so as not to cause her to prick the little girl's shin.

Taking Clint by the hand, Jennifer all but dragged him out through the door and off to the side so they weren't blocking the shop's entrance. "I really am glad you're all right. Now did you really talk to both of those men?"

"Yep. I even got to turn my back on Teaghan. That didn't go over too well at all."

Clint took a moment to fill her in on what he'd been doing since the last time they'd been together. Although it had only been an hour or so since they were eating

together, he'd done more than most people in that town
did in a lifetime. In fact, Jennifer seemed impressed that
he'd gotten Brandon and Teaghan together and lived to
tell about it.

"How could you stand being around those two?" Jennifer asked.

"Actually, Brandon wasn't as bad as I was expecting."

"He's just trying to pull the wool over your eyes. Don't
let him."

They'd started walking down the boardwalk, attracting
attention every step of the way. The locals in the area
stared at Clint more than anything else, but didn't try to
approach him or say anything to catch his eye. He noticed
them just fine, all the same.

Shaking his head, Clint said, "I don't think so. The
man's full of it, that's for sure, but not any more than
most politicians I've met. He's not the real danger here.
Teaghan's the one to worry about."

"Well I agree with that."

"Was it true what he told me about what happened to
the sheriff?"

She lowered her eyes and nodded slowly. "Yes. Every
horrible word of it. I was there, just like most of the town.
I saw that building go up in flames and heard Sam Bowdrie hollering from inside. Me and plenty of others wanted
to help, but those killers working for Teaghan kept us
back. Some were even killed when they got too close."

Both of them were quiet for the next couple of minutes.
Finally, Clint spotted a familiar place and led Jennifer in
that direction. Paco's Cantina was just the way he remembered it, right down to the unsavory characters milling
around outside its doors at all hours of the day.

It was the kind of place where the regulars knew to

keep their distance unless invited and found it healthier to mind their own business. Besides all that, Clint wanted to do some checking of his own and that was just the kind of place he wanted to start.

THIRTY-FOUR

Jennifer listened to Clint talk without interrupting him
once. As he spoke, she took in every word and nodded
to let him know she understood. He didn't talk to her for
very long, but by the time he was finished, she felt as
though she was being overwhelmed.

"So what are you saying?" she asked once she realized
he was finished. "Is this your way of getting rid of the
killers in this town?"

Clint nodded. "It's what I should have done three years
ago. Do you understand what I need you to do?"

"Yes, but I'm not sure I can do it. Not in just one day."

"This is a small town and you know pretty much everyone in it, don't you?"

"Well, yes, but—"

"But nothing." Clint's voice had taken on a sudden
edge. It was sharp enough to cut through the doubt that
had been forming in Jennifer's mind and let her know he
truly meant business. "I'll try to do my part to set things
right here, but I'm not about to do it all. That's what went
wrong last time, and this is the best way I can think of to
make up for it. If you've got a better idea, then let's hear

it. Otherwise, I think this could just make things work out all around."

Although she seemed a little frightened, Jennifer straightened her back and gave Clint one crisp nod. "You're right. This sounds a little frightening, but it could work."

"It has worked in other towns real well," Clint told her. "Believe me."

"You mean other towns have problems like this and work it out the way you were describing?"

"It's not a general rule, but yeah. You'd be surprised how common a problem a man like Teaghan and Brandon are. They're kind of like rats or cockroaches . . . or maybe even those politicians I was telling you about."

Jennifer smiled at that and laughed in spite of the nervousness she was feeling.

Reaching out to brush his hand along her face, Clint said, "It's nice to see you smile again. I was starting to wonder if I'd taken that away for good."

She shook her head. "Actually, I've been smiling a lot more since you've been around."

For a moment, they looked at each other, staring into each other's eyes and letting their faces drift closer together. Just when Clint could feel the heat from her lips near his mouth, he blinked and felt her pull away. He was stunned for a moment, simply because she'd moved so quickly.

"Was it something I said?" he asked.

"No. Not at all. I just . . . I really should be going. There's a lot I need to do, so I'd better get started."

Although she reached out to touch his hand, Jennifer turned her back on him and began walking down the street. Clint watched her for a few moments, wondering if she was truly upset or if she was simply flustered that they were in the middle of a public place rather than somewhere more private.

He knew that if she kept her head down and walked as fast as she could, she was probably embarrassed and possibly even a bit regretful that she'd let him get so close. But, on the other hand, if she slowed down and looked at him over her shoulder, there was definitely more of a chance that she was as interested in him as he was in her.

Clint waited and watched. He stood still and didn't say a word, watching her walk away from the cantina toward the town's more respectable business district. Finally, after no more than ten or fifteen seconds, she slowed and glanced over her shoulder.

Smiling, Clint gave her a wave, which sent Jennifer even quicker on her way down the street.

As much as he would have liked to watch Jennifer's attractive backside wiggle when she walked, Clint had other business to tend to. He'd originally intended to call on Sofia, but had not even gotten around to checking to see if she was even in town any longer or if she'd moved on. That would still have to wait, though. There were a whole lot of people to talk to and very little time. Suddenly, he felt like one of those politicians that seemed to be coming up more and more in conversation. Unlike those shysters, Clint had every intention of keeping his promises.

THIRTY-FIVE

It was well into dusk by the time Clint was able to check in on Sofia. Throughout the afternoon, he'd asked a few of the people he'd talked to about her, but he always seemed to pick either someone who didn't move in her circles or just plain didn't know her. He'd come across a few who recognized the name, but that was about it.

Like many other puzzles that he couldn't solve right away, this one nagged at the back of his head like a gnat that was trapped in his hatband. Finally, Clint decided to satisfy his curiosity and just go to the last place where he knew she'd lived.

The little narrow house was still there, as was the general store that had been beside it. As soon as he spotted her door, Clint felt as though it had only been a few weeks since he'd been there. Already, he could picture the inside of the place as well as every nook and cranny of the upstairs that they'd explored in such a memorable way.

Before he knew it, Clint had jumped up onto the boardwalk and was reaching out to rap on the door. His knuckles banged on the wood in a quick rhythm, and he could hear footsteps approaching from the other side. He didn't

have to wait for more than a few more seconds before the
door was pulled open and he could set his eyes on the
lovely face that had been in his thoughts so much as of
late.

"Hello," the woman said, her eyes taking in the sight
of Clint with no small amount of interest.

Her features were definitely beautiful and her body
looked stunning even in her simple dress, but she was
most definitely not Sofia. Sure, it had been a few years
since he'd seen her last, but there was no way that this
was the same woman he'd been with the last time he'd
been in town. For that to be possible, she would have had
to have shrunk a foot and changed the color of her skin
and hair.

The woman standing in front of him now was the color
of smooth chocolate. Her full, soft lips remained in a
smile and widened as she got a better look at him.

"You're Clint Adams, aren't you?" she asked.

Trying not to look too surprised, Clint tipped his hat
and said, "I sure am."

"I knew it. I recognized your face and heard you were
in town. What can I do for you?"

"I didn't catch your name."

"Where are my manners? Please, come in." She
stepped aside and held the door open for him. As she
waited for him to enter, she quickly straightened her skirt
and fussed with her hair, making the little differences that
only she or another woman would have noticed. "My
name's Sandra Rigsby."

"Pleased to meet you, Sandra. Thanks for giving me a
moment of your time."

"No problem, Mr. Adams. I've heard all about you."

Clint stepped into the home and took a look around. It
was like stepping into half of a memory. The basic struc-

ture was the same, things like the room divisions and of course the stairs in the back, but the details had changed. There was different furniture and the different feel of the new owner, which made it her own.

Before allowing himself to stare at the room and ignore the woman who owned it, Clint shifted his gaze back to Sandra and smiled. "I hope I'm not intruding at this hour, but I was wondering if you might help me."

"If I can, I'd be more than happy to. Would you like to sit down?"

Before he could answer, Clint found himself being led to one of three chairs positioned next to a small fireplace. "How long have you lived here?" he asked, taking the seat he was offered.

Sandra stopped in front of her own chair and kneaded her hands while thinking. "Oh, I'd say a little over a year and a half."

"Did you know who lived here before you?"

"Yes," she answered in a voice that was noticeably different than what Clint had been hearing before. The wringing of her hands sped up and she lowered her eyes as if she was afraid of what Clint might ask next.

"Sofia was the last one to own it, wasn't she? Or was there someone else in the meantime?"

"No, it was Sofia."

"I was just wondering where I might be able to find her."

Lifting her chin, Sandra took a breath and said, "She's in the Lord's hands now, Mr. Adams."

"What?"

"She's dead."

THIRTY-SIX

As those words washed over him, Clint felt the need to finally sit himself down into the chair he'd merely been standing in front of this whole time. Even with his weight off his feet, Clint still felt as though he might fall over. Sandra got them both some water, which helped them both get their second winds.

"She's dead?" he asked. "What happened?"

"It was about two years ago. She moved out and was all set to take off for California when Brandon Morris comes into town."

Clint felt the hairs on his neck stand on end.

"She had words with him and even stood up to him more than once," Sandra continued. "Folks said it was because of all the time she spent with you that she became such a fighter. I knew her for a while and she always had spirit, but being with you and seeing the things you done really meant something to her.

"Anyway, she damn near put Mr. Morris in his place all by herself. That's when Mr. Teaghan came and everything changed." While she'd been talking fondly before, Sandra's voice now sounded more apprehensive. It was even a bit fearful. "Things changed for all of us. She was there to watch the fire that killed Sheriff Bowdrie." She looked up at Clint as if to check that he knew what she was talking about.

Clint nodded, which was enough to let her move on.

"After that, she tried getting folks to take him on themselves," Sandra said. "They wouldn't. She tried and tried, but they wouldn't budge. I'm ashamed to say, I was one of them. Mr. Teaghan's a killer and those men that work for him . . . they're worse.

"Well, Sofia would hear none of it. She said that there won't always be someone around to help. Someone like . . . well . . . like you," Sandra added, glancing over at Clint. "She tried to stand up to Mr. Teaghan, but she couldn't even get close enough to speak her mind."

"What happened?" Clint asked grimly.

"One of Mr. Teaghan's men, the tall one who looks like Death himself. He shot her dead right on his doorstep." Sandra needed a moment to collect herself before she could continue. The tears were at the corners of her eyes and she dabbed them away with the corner of a handkerchief. By the way she moved and the expression on her face, the grief was nothing new to her. Those tears had been shed before.

Pushing the sorrow back once again, Sandra looked Clint in the eyes and told him, "Sofia was one of Mr. Teaghan's examples. He said she was a lesson that everyone needed to learn if they was going to live here. There haven't been many more lessons since then. Well, not since today."

Clint stood up. Suddenly, he felt the need to get out of that house. He also felt the need to get out of that whole town, but managed to choke it all back and keep a relatively normal expression on his face. Sandra had gotten up as well, so he extended a hand to her.

He held his hand out for less than a second before starting to feel foolish. Instead, he took her in his arms and gave her a hug.

"I'm sorry to hear about Sofia," Clint told her. "I'm sorry about everything."

"Don't be sorry. That bastard that killed her is the one who should feel sorry. And so should that bastard Teaghan. They should all be sorry for all the evil they done." She looked him in the eye and added, "Only thing is that I don't think men like that can feel sorry for anything. Otherwise, they wouldn't even be able to live with themselves."

Clint's voice was cold as stone when he told her, "Don't worry about any of that. I'm here now. I'll make them sorry they ever heard of this town."

". . . did everything you told me and you wouldn't believe it," Jennifer chattered. "All I had to do was mention your name and they were ready to go. They're behind us, Clint. All of them."

Clint nodded as though he were listening to her from a great distance. "That's great."

Jennifer recoiled as though she'd been slapped. They were back in her room above the shop, and Clint was in a mood she found very surprising. "I don't . . . don't understand."

"It just seems I've done more harm to this town than good. I just found out that I caused a woman to rush into someplace she didn't belong and get killed for her troubles. This place was better off with some loudmouth like Dutch Dreyman as your only worry. Now look at it. Everywhere I turn is blood and death."

Clint was sitting on the edge of her bed, so Jennifer came around to stand directly in front of him. The sun was long gone and the sky was a mixture of black, dark blue and some slivers of purple. Light from the stars and moon blended with the single lantern in the room, which accentuated the seriousness of her expression.

"Look here," she said, kneeling down so that she could look straight into his eyes. "Dutch was an asshole and someone needed to stand up to him. You did and showed all of us the way things should be done. Brandon Morris and Jeremy Teaghan would have come through here with or without you having come before.

"I don't know why they came here. Maybe Teaghan was right and maybe we all did need to learn a lesson or two. But they would have come through here just the same, and if you hadn't been here to take care of Dutch Dreyman, I know that Teaghan sure as hell would have. Dutch was a bastard, but someone like Teaghan would have chewed him up, spit him out, and then we'd be right back here.

"You made a difference then, Clint, and you're making one now. I saw the looks in people's eyes, and they're ready to back your plan every step of the way. They wouldn't do it when other folks tried to light a fire under them, but they'll do it for you."

Jennifer leaned in even closer. She started to say more, but instead held Clint's face in her hands and kissed him gently on the lips. Although there were things she wanted to say, she stopped a second time as another need took over.

She kissed him again. This time, however, her lips parted and her tongue ran gently over Clint's lips. Reflexively, Clint's mouth opened as well and their tongues brushed together just enough for them to sample the other's taste.

Her lips closed around Clint's bottom lip until she slowly let him break away from her. With her face still close enough to Clint's that they could feel each other's warmth, she said, "They believe in you, Clint. Everyone I talked to today believes in you and so do I. Doesn't that count for something?"

"Yeah," Clint whispered. "It counts for a lot."

Jennifer smiled as her fingers slid along his face and kept moving down until she could start unbuttoning his shirt. Clint felt himself being pushed farther back onto the bed. Before long, Jennifer was pushing him all the way down and was crawling on top of him.

Jennifer tugged at Clint's pants until they came undone and she was able to slide them off of him completely. His cock was rigid and waiting for her and her hands instantly wrapped around it. While stroking him up and down, she let out a breath as she felt his hands begin to peel her clothes off of her body.

As soon as the material was free from her flesh, Clint could appreciate her curves even more. Her breasts were full and just the right size to fill his hands when he cupped them. Her nipples were small and hard with anticipation. Rolling them between his thumb and forefinger was enough to get Jennifer to moan just loud enough for him to hear.

She slid herself toward the foot of the bed, brushing her skin over Clint's flesh until her feet touched the floor. When he propped himself up to look at her, Clint saw that her eyes hadn't left him and she was just waiting for him to turn all his attention toward her.

Slowly, Jennifer took hold of her dress that Clint had tugged down to her waist in a bunch. Once the skirts had dropped back down to cover her, she reached down with both hands and took hold of the material. From there, she lifted it slowly, all the way over her head so she could drop it behind her and kick it back with one foot.

Clint rolled onto his side so he could be more comfortable for the show. She was only wearing a slip, which was just a skirt that clung to her body thanks to the sweat they'd already worked up. Taking hold of the slip, she moved her hips back and forth while pulling the slip up, teasing him by letting him see more and more of her naked body.

Finally, just when she thought Clint was about to burst, Jennifer let the slip drop down to her feet, leaving only her small underpants to go. Turning around, she peeled that last bit of clothing down, exposing the delicious curve of her buttocks while peeking at him over her shoulder.

Just watching her, Clint felt every muscle in his body aching to be closer to her. His penis was so erect that it ached to be inside of her, but when he tried to move toward her, he was stopped by a playful wagging of her finger.

"Not yet," she warned in a low, seductive voice. "I want to get closer to you first."

With a bit of gentle prodding, Jennifer got him to lean back onto the bed with his legs dangling over the edge. She started with her knees on the floor, pressing her body against him and slowly rubbing herself up and along him while her hands snaked out in advance.

Clint leaned back, savoring the feel of her moving up his body, yet dying to feel even more than that. He closed his eyes so he could concentrate on nothing but the sensation of her skin against his own. The soft, firm curves of her body slid over his legs and then up to his thighs. After waiting for what seemed like forever, he felt her fingers slide over his cock as her body kept right on moving.

To his disappointment, her hand left him, but was immediately replaced by something warmer and much softer. He felt her tongue glide over his shaft, moistening his skin with long, deliberate strokes. When he opened his eyes again, she was staring up at him, pressing his cock between her breasts and sliding them up and down.

Her nipples were getting harder by the second, and so was he.

THIRTY-SEVEN

Jennifer leaned her head back and savored the feel of Clint's rigid penis between her breasts. Letting her instincts take over, she crawled up on top of him and felt him move beneath her so he could get all the way onto the bed.

Clint reached up to cup her breasts. His hands felt so good on her, covering her and massaging her with strength as well as gentleness. She placed her hands on top of his, arching her back and straddling him with her legs spread open wide. All they had to do was shift their hips and he was inside of her. His cock was so hard that it just took a single push of his hips for Clint to slide it between her wet, waiting lips.

They both let out a breath and felt the tension that had been building up inside of them start to melt away. As Clint pushed up into her, he slid his hands over Jennifer's nipples, moving his palms all the way down until he could take hold of her hips.

Now that his hands had moved, Jennifer discovered her own hands were still on her breasts. She kept them there, feeling natural and completely unashamed to pleasure herself with her own touch. Clint was hard inside of her, filling her up with his thick column of flesh until he was buried deep inside of her.

Jennifer's eyes were clenched shut and her lips were moving as if to form silent words. Her fingers moved slowly over her nipples, the sight of which sent an excited chill down Clint's spine. When she opened her eyes again, she was just in time to see Clint sit up and take hold of her, rolling so that they were both lying on their sides.

Moving however felt natural, Jennifer raised one leg and draped it over Clint's side, allowing him to pump freely between her legs as she reached out to run her fingers through his hair. His face was tense with the effort of his motions and the pleasure he felt was becoming greater with every thrust.

Finally, Clint let out a long groan as he drove his cock into her as deep as it would go. The impact of their bodies shook the bed and caused her pussy to clench around him. Jennifer's breaths were coming in quick gasps now, and her face bore an expression as though she was pleading with him not to stop.

Clint pushed into her one more time before laying her onto her back and settling on top of her. Jennifer let her arms stretch out on the bed and spread her legs open wide with one foot digging into the blankets. When she felt Clint's hands close over her own, she handed over all the control to him so she could savor the feeling of him pumping in and out of her.

Drinking in the sight of the beautiful woman underneath him, Clint let his eyes roam freely over her body, drinking in the sight of Jennifer's naked skin as she reacted to every little thing he did to her. Her full, red lips were curled into a smile and her head tossed from side to side as if in the middle of an intense dream.

Suddenly, Jennifer arched her back and started to squirm beneath him. "Don't stop," she whispered.

But there was no danger of that. Clint felt his own pleasure building to a climax and could tell by the expression on her face that Jennifer was feeling the very same thing.

"Oh, god," she said a little louder. "Don't stop!" She was screaming now, completely wrapped up in the moment and absorbed in the intense pleasure Clint was giving to her. Without thinking, she pulled her hands out from Clint's and pressed them against her breasts. She held his hands on her as he thrust into her again and again in slower, yet more powerful motions.

When her orgasm finally came, Jennifer was pumping her hips in time to Clint's thrusts and her feet were pushing down against the bed. Clint's own body was awash in such erotic pleasure that he truly thought he might burst.

Now in the grip of her climax, Jennifer clenched her eyes shut and became very quiet. All of her energy seemed to be focused on the pleasure coursing through her. And when it finally reached its peak, she let out a barely audible cry and finally relaxed her muscles.

Clint had slowed his pace a bit to prolong the moment. Once he saw that Jennifer was opening her eyes beneath him, he shifted his hips so that his shaft was pressed against her clit and slid all the way in one last time. That was enough to push her into a second orgasm and when her pussy tightened around him, it sent Clint straight over the brink.

They lay there for a moment after the sensation had swept through them. Both of them were spent from their lovemaking, yet neither of them wanted to move from their spot.

THIRTY-EIGHT

Clint and Jennifer weren't the only ones who'd chosen to spend that night in that particular way. In a room on the top floor of a small, nondescript storefront, another man and woman were locked in a tangle of arms and legs with the scent of sex heavy in the air.

Jeremy Teaghan gritted his teeth as he pumped furiously into the naked body of the slim redhead in front of him. She clawed at the sheets like an animal, lowering her head and arching her back as he thrust into her again and again.

When she lifted her head to try and let out a sound, she felt Teaghan's fingers sift through her hair and make a tight, painful fist. He pulled back without regard to how it might feel, wrenching her head back to an almost fatal angle.

He looked down at her like she was something he'd conquered and was now pillaging at will. Even though she'd come to his bed willingly, the redhead wasn't being treated like a guest. In fact, she wanted to scream but knew that would only make him want to hurt her more and worse. Besides, she knew that the pain would let up soon enough and the pleasure would fill her once again.

Sure enough, just like every time they'd gotten together, Teaghan let his grip relax and focused on his own
pleasure. He took hold of her hips and pulled her strongly
to him as he thrust forward.

This was the part that Allie liked best and the redhead
showed it by pulling the sheets from the mattress and
letting out a cry that sounded almost feral. She bucked
against him, so familiar with his patterns that she knew
he was going to climax at any second. Her own body was
tingling with anticipation and when she felt his grip on
her shoulders, she braced herself for the final blows.

Teaghan's body pumped forward, his hands clamped
on her shoulders so he could pull her closer while thrust-
ing with his hips. She was dripping wet between her legs,
which allowed him to thrust as hard as he wanted until
he finally exploded inside of her.

Allie was screaming and tossing her red hair from side
to side, enjoying the tingles of her own orgasm until they
quickly faded into a comfortable flush of color just beneath her skin. As soon as the motion stopped between
her thighs, she crawled forward and rolled onto her side,
running her fingers along her stomach and between her
legs.

She felt the need to touch herself after Teaghan was
finished. It might have been awkward or erotic depending
on the inclination of the person watching her. But Allie
didn't have to worry about that since Teaghan was too
wrapped up in getting his clothes back on to watch her
do anything.

"So," Teaghan said, his mind already on to bigger and
better things, "what have you heard from Morris?"

Allie opened her eyes and took a moment to regain her
focus. Her hands were still lingering over her body so it

took a moment for her to figure out what he was talking about. Then again, the man didn't have many tracks in his mind, so it wasn't too difficult of a task.

"Not much," she replied. "In fact, nothing at all. I swear I don't know why you waste the money paying to keep my services."

"Spying on that dullard Brandon Morris is only one of your services, my dear." The way he spoke to her was full of smug self-assuredness. There wasn't the slightest bit of tenderness to be found. "Besides, there is potential for him to be a problem. Especially now that he's gotten close to Clint Adams."

Just hearing that name was enough to make Allie want to touch herself all over again. Deciding to save that for another time, she got up and started collecting her clothes. "He does a lot of business behind our back, but nothing you should be concerned about."

"Enough to pay you more than I do?" Teaghan asked.

The question had come so quickly and at a time when she was so distracted that Allie damn near blurted out the truth.

"No," she said instead. "I doubt he even knows I'm looking in on him. He's too wrapped up in his own affairs."

"Is he a friend of Clint Adams?"

"No," she said with a laugh. "He was just as surprised to see him come back into town as you were. Well," she corrected herself when she saw the stern look on Teaghan's face, "he was as surprised as everyone else in town was."

Teaghan studied her for a few moments as he put the finishing touches on himself. He buttoned his buttons and straightened his tie without once taking his eyes off of her. When she turned around after cinching up her dress,

Allie looked a bit surprised and, Teaghan thought, more than that.

"Well, I guess it doesn't rightly matter," he told her. "Adams is nothing more than a gunfighter. He's been here before and he's welcome to come back again just so long as he knows his place here. That's what I've got to teach him."

"And what if he just leaves like he said he would?"

"Then the lesson was already learned. But he won't leave. I had Dave keep an eye on him. He and that blond seamstress have been making the rounds, whispering in ears all over the place."

"Really? What have they been saying?"

Having just buckled on his gun belt, Teaghan took a breath and drew his pistol in less time than it took for Allie to blink. Surging forward like a cobra with its fangs bared, Teaghan reached out with both hands. One hand gripped Allie by the neck and the other jammed the gun up underneath her chin.

"That," he hissed, "is exactly the type of thing I pay you to find out."

All the color had drained from her skin and her hands were fluttering nervously in front of her, unsure of what to do next. When Teaghan thumbed back the hammer, she felt the steel under her jaw twitch and felt her entire body go cold.

"And did you hear any of these whispers?" Teaghan asked. "Or were you too busy spending the money I gave you?"

"I swear, I didn't hear anything."

"Lies. I can smell 'em coming from you. Right now, it's best to admit you done wrong and tell me what I want to hear. Lesson learned. Otherwise, I'll have to make you an example to others."

Tears were coming down her face now. If she had the energy, Allie would have started to tremble. As it was, she could barely keep herself breathing.

"B-Brandon paid me t-to keep quiet."

"So he knew about our arrangement?"

"No. H-he figured one of the g-girls was talking to you and sent us a-all away with extra money for the d-day to make up for it. I d-don't know what he'll do next."

Teaghan studied the redhead's face for a moment or two. For Allie, those few moments seemed to drag out like they lasted a year each. Once he'd seen what he'd wanted to see, Teaghan softened his features and started to nod.

"You know something?" he said calmly. "I believe you."

Allie's relief could be felt like a cool breeze coming through the room.

"Well," Teaghan added, "I believe some of it anyway. For instance, I believe that Morris was smart enough to see through a stupid whore like you and that you didn't hear shit from him that could be useful."

Before she could start begging, Allie heard a muffled roar and felt a brief blast of heat move through her head. After that, she couldn't feel much of anything. Not even the floor as her dead body was dropped off just inside The Rusty Spur a few minutes later.

THIRTY-NINE

The next morning came, same as any other, and the town of Cielo Grande went about its business as if this day was no different from the one before. But as Clint ate breakfast and met with a few more locals, he could feel that there was most definitely a difference that went down to the dirt below the wooden boardwalks.

Folks were nervous and scared, yet still ready to act. Clint could tell all of this because in the past day, he'd personally spoken to or met with nearly everyone who lived there. And the ones he hadn't met were the ones that Jennifer had talked to. Between the both of them, Clint and Jennifer had spread the word to the whole town or, at least, to everyone in the town who was supposed to know what was going on.

Clint felt a connection to Cielo Grande this morning more than ever. His connection ran deeper than it did to places where he'd spent more time or knew more people. That connection came because he'd been the one to make a difference in that place as well as in the lives of practically everyone who lived there.

He'd been the one to tip the balance and he was set to do it again.

Although they were nervous, the faces he saw looked him in the eye and returned Clint's nod with a strong one of their own. In that simple gesture, Clint could tell a great many things. Just as he would read someone sitting across from him at a poker game, Clint could see the strength and resolve in all those faces.

They were ready.

As for Clint himself, he was always ready. He had to live that way or he wouldn't live very long at all.

He wished there could have been a simpler way to resolve all of this, but there simply wasn't. He'd tried it the easy way and now it was time to change his own way of thinking as well. In that respect, Clint realized that the town of Cielo Grande just might have tipped his own balance as well.

It was afternoon when Clint finally met up with a familiar face that wasn't scared or even the slightest bit nervous.

"How are you feeling?" Jennifer asked as she walked up to where Clint was waiting.

Standing with his back against the post of the general store, Clint looked up to the sky and nodded. It was a hot day, but pretty much what he would expect for that time of year. The heat felt good on his skin, though. It warmed him without burning in much the same way as the sun beat down on him without hammering him into the ground.

"I'm doing pretty well," he replied. "You?"

"I feel really good. It's kind of strange because I should be nervous, but I'm not. Well, I am, but . . ." She took a moment to look up at the sky as well. When she looked down, the resolve Clint had seen in her eyes was even stronger. "But as nervous as I am, it feels good to finally be here. After today, things are going to be set right."

"I'm glad someone sees things that way."

"It's not just me," she said, reaching out to turn Clint's face so he was looking straight at her. After placing a kiss on Clint's lips, she said, "It's everyone. We believe in you, Clint Adams. All of us do."

Clint wished he could buy in to the optimism in Jennifer's words and expression. He wished he could believe so strongly in himself the way all those locals did. He was the one allowing them to be scared, but ready, instead of just plain scared.

But Clint knew why they looked at him that way. He knew why they could let themselves believe so strongly in what he told them despite their fears. They saw him as the Gunsmith. A legend. The man who'd come to them once before and delivered them from evil.

Clint smiled when he thought of it that way because it seemed so overly dramatic. But to them, it wasn't over the top. For the moment, that's the way it had to be.

Even though Clint knew he was just a man who could bleed, make mistakes and get himself hurt or killed, he had to let the rest of the town keep believing he was more than that. At least, that had to last a little longer.

"What are you thinking about?" Jennifer asked. She'd been staring into Clint's eyes this whole time, yet he'd only now become aware of it.

Pushing himself away from the post that he'd been leaning against, Clint turned to face the street that had only recently become devoid of people. "I'm thinking it's time to get to work."

FORTY

As Clint walked down Mesa Street, he felt all the eyes staring intently at him. He couldn't see those eyes, since most of their owners had made themselves scarce. Apparently, news of Clint's run-in with Teaghan had spread to every house and every store.

The emptiness didn't bother him, however, since he'd been partially responsible for it. One of the things he and Jennifer had told everybody was when Clint meant to have another talk with Teaghan and that smart folks would do well to be somewhere else when it happened.

Clint was glad to see the streets empty out the closer he got to the corner of Military Avenue. That meant that if things did go bad, there wouldn't be anyone around who could get hurt. Also, Clint had Teaghan figured as the type of man who would rather perform in front of an audience.

His walk wasn't made completely on his own, however. There was someone following in his tracks about twenty paces behind him. And as far as Clint could tell, that other person had been there for a good block and a half.

By the time he rounded the corner and started walking along Military, Clint could hear the distinct sound of the other man's boots as they kept in perfect step with him. To his ears, that extra set of steps echoed down the street like a shot in an empty room. Each one of them crunched louder against the dirt as the man behind him realized he'd been found out.

Even though he knew he wasn't going to be a surprise to Clint, that other man kept following him. The point was no longer to go unnoticed. The point had become to let Clint know that he wasn't about to sneak up on anyone or go anywhere without being watched.

That was just fine by Clint.

Every one of his senses was stretched to the breaking point. His eyes darted back and forth, up and down, searching for anything that was out of place or anyone staring back at him from any window, door, or alleyway. His ears followed not only the steps behind him, but any other sound apart from the wind blowing through the town.

Even the tips of his fingers and toes were on the alert, tingling with the anticipation of whatever was about to happen. As much as Clint had thought this over and planned it out, he knew there was no way in hell he could foresee every possible way this could end up.

He had his hopes and preferences, but the world has a way of turning however it wants to turn without regard for what any man wanted or hoped.

There was someone watching him from the second-floor window of a hotel close by. Clint recognized the face as one of the men who'd been with Teaghan the day before. It was an older man's face, covered with a dark beard with flecks of gray. The sun glinted off a gun barrel resting on the windowsill and Clint had no doubt in his mind that the bearded man would pull his trigger without hesitation.

There was another man standing in the doorway of the building two lots away from where Teaghan would be waiting. It was another of Teaghan's men wearing the same dark suit with matching dark overcoat. It was hard to tell in the sunlight if that suit was dark blue or black. When he saw Clint looking at him, the younger man returned his gaze with a pair of threatening, light-colored eyes.

Without breaking stride, Clint held the other man's stare until the guy in the dark suit removed his hat to reveal the clean-shaven scalp underneath. The younger man swept his arm and hat forward and to the side, motioning dramatically for Clint to continue down the road toward Teaghan's place.

Clint stifled a laugh and kept walking, as if thumbing his nose at the younger man for making it seem as if he'd needed his permission to do so.

As he walked past the building next to Teaghan's, Clint saw the door to that unmarked storefront open and a pair of figures step outside. The first was a man wearing a dark goatee and a cold look that made his eyes seem dead. His mouth formed into a passive frown that was neither sad nor worried. After taking a few steps through the door, he swept his black coat open to reveal the holster strapped around his waist and to his leg. After that, he practically turned to stone. The only trace of movement was when the wind tugged at the edges of his clothes.

Teaghan walked through the door and came to a stop at the precise moment that Clint took his place in the street before him. Although the holster was clearly visible around his waist, Teaghan didn't move as though he wanted to display it or the weapon it held. Instead, he hooked his thumbs in his waistband and stretched his neck while taking in a long, deep breath of desert air.

"It's been one hell of a day, hasn't it, Mr. Adams?" Teaghan said. "Looks like it'll be one hell of a night as well."

Clint didn't answer. He just took in the street around him and watched to see what would happen next. The man following him had stopped a few paces back. Clint didn't have to look in that direction to know which man had been following him. Just to be safe, however, he gave a quick glance anyway.

The tall, gaunt figure in the black suit and coat was staring back at him. His skin hung on him like worn leather and his eyes were dark, smoldering slits.

That would be Dave. Just the man Clint had been expecting.

"Did you stop to say good-bye before you left, Mr. Adams?" Teaghan asked. "Very courteous of you."

"You're partly right," Clint said. "I came to say good-bye, but I'm not the one that's leaving."

FORTY-ONE

Teaghan pulled in another long, deliberate breath. This time he didn't seem to be sampling the air as much as he was letting out the steam that had been building up inside of him. He let the breath pass by his teeth while slowly shaking his head.

"I thought you were smarter than this, Mr. Adams. I thought you were a man I could deal with as a gentleman."

"Well you show me a gentleman and I'll deal with him," Clint replied. "Until then, I guess I'll have to deal with you."

"Juvenile quips weren't exactly what I expected from you."

"Yeah, well sometimes they just fit the moment."

"Not this one. This is the moment where you leave this town behind you and move on to another one. Surely there must be some other places for a man such as yourself. Places with more excitement." Teaghan's eyes brightened for a second. "You're a gambler, aren't you? Try San Francisco or even Tombstone. There's some fine games that are more suited to a player like you."

"I tried walking away from here. It didn't work out too well. Seems that a bunch of rats moved in and infested the place."

The smirk that had been on Teaghan's face froze right where it was. It seemed to hang there like smoke in the sky after the train had already moved along. When it faded, the smile melted from his lips to leave an ugly sneer in its place.

"You're a man to be respected, that's for sure," Teaghan said. "But I've already cut you plenty of slack and you just keep testing me. If you're not open to courtesy, then how about something more straightforward? Leave. Now."

"Or what?" Clint asked. "You'll make me another example? The people in this town have had their fill of you and it's time for you to go."

"Telling me that is the sheriff's job, isn't it?"

"Yeah. It is. And now you're the one testing me. Sam Bowdrie was a good man and because of you, he's still lying in a pile of ash for everyone to see."

"And what do you want me to do about that?"

"Clean up the mess you made," Clint replied evenly. "You'll sift through those ashes until you find every man that died in that fire. You'll then bury whatever you find so Sam Bowdrie and his men can rest properly. They deserve that much and you, not anyone else or any of your men, will do it." Now it was Clint's turn to smirk. "That's the example I'd like to set."

Teaghan cocked his head as he studied Clint, waiting as if he half-expected Clint to admit that he was kidding. But all he got was a glare that was every bit as serious as his own, which was something Teaghan was obviously not used to seeing.

"You're serious?" Teaghan asked.

Clint nodded.

"Then you've wasted your time here, Mr. Adams. And you've wasted the one chance I was generous enough to give you. Since you're still in my town after I asked you to leave, I'll have to have you escorted out by my men.

"Is there anything else you'd like to say, or would you just like to fetch your horse and start riding?"

Clint looked around, taking in the street and the other faces he could see. Apart from Teaghan and his men, there weren't any other living souls to be seen. All the other men in dark suits were standing exactly where they'd been the last time he'd looked at them. It seemed as though their muscles didn't function unless Teaghan gave the order.

"All right then," Teaghan said after a few more moments of silence. "If this is the way you want to play it, I'm willing to go along." He turned to the man standing in the doorway of the neighboring building, snapped his fingers and said, "Warren, come see Mr. Adams to his horse and out of my town."

The younger man in the doorway stepped forward and dropped down from the boardwalk. The moment his boots hit the dirt, he started walking swiftly toward Clint. After only a few steps, he pulled aside his coat and hooked the edge of it behind his holster to free up his gun. When he did that, his expression took on a harder edge, as though he was expecting Clint to flinch at the sight of his weapon.

"Make this easy on yerself," Warren said. "And you might just walk out of here in one piece."

Clint shifted so that he was facing more toward Warren, but without taking his eyes off of the other men. So far, none of the other three was making a move although Clint was certain they were ready to jump in and lend a hand at the drop of a hat.

Warren stopped just outside of Clint's arm's reach and waited for a moment. Seeing that Clint still wasn't going to move, he glanced over to Teaghan one last time and immediately received a nod from his boss.

Clint had spotted the scabbard on Warren's gun belt the moment the younger man had opened his coat. The knife was kept on the opposite side as the gun and was situated slightly back so as not to be as visible as the firearm. All Clint needed to see, however, was the tip of leather and glint of metal for him to know what else Warren was hiding.

The younger man stepped forward with one leg, positioning himself sideways with his holster facing out toward Clint. His gun hand dropped to the firearm's handle and his other hand darted completely out of view.

Having figured out exactly what Warren meant to do, Clint made it look as though he was playing straight into it. He focused his eyes on Warren's gun arm while lowering his own hand to the modified Colt at his side. As Warren moved forward, Clint kept going for his gun and squaring off like he meant to draw and fire.

But Warren didn't mean to draw his gun. Moving his hand toward it, even throwing open his coat to display the weapon had all been feints to pull Clint's attention away from the younger man's true weapon of choice. Unfortunately for Warren, Clint had studied body language as it applied to fights just as much as he had in poker tells.

Warren was a knife fighter. He had the flourishes and hardware to prove it. He appeared to be a damn good knife fighter, but he was just a little too cocky. It was a common mistake of youth. Too bad Warren wouldn't live long enough to learn from his mistake.

Warren's hand slapped onto the grip of his pistol and

made a fist around the handle while his other hand had already plucked the knife from its scabbard and was slashing around toward Clint. Everything his gun hand did was out for all to see, while his knife hand remained hidden beneath his coat.

Clint didn't need to see Warren's knife hand to know what it was up to. He anticipated the move and made one of his own to compensate. Plucking the Colt from its holster, he brought it up in a quick whisper of motion.

Instead of leveling the barrel to take aim, Clint made a feint of his own in that direction before swinging the pistol across to intercept the knife he knew to be coming. Sure enough, Warren's blade sliced outward and sparked against the side of Clint's gun.

Judging by the look on Warren's face, he was still expecting to see the knife sink into flesh even as it was deflected. He quickly figured out that Clint had been ahead of him. Even so, he wasn't quick enough to stop what happened next.

Clint closed his hand around Warren's wrist, twisted it sharply and forced the younger man to drop his blade. Next, he swung the Colt back across and upward, catching Warren directly beneath the chin and snapping his head back with a dull crunch.

Even before Warren's back hit the dirt, Clint was turning back around to check on the other gunmen.

He was too late, however.

They were already gone.

FORTY-TWO

The first one he spotted was the man with the goatee. That one had left Teaghan's side and was charging down the boardwalk on Clint's left. His eyes were still cold and focused as he reached for the gun at his side and drew the weapon in one fluid motion.

Clint's body reacted without needing his brain to think it over. Just seeing the man with the goatee draw his gun was enough for Clint to respond in kind, shifting his aim and squeezing the Colt's trigger.

Even as the Colt barked and spat out its smoky plume, the man with the goatee had already leapt off the walkway and onto the street. He folded his legs beneath him as he landed to throw himself into a forward roll. Since his face was still stony and expressionless, it was impossible to say whether or not Clint's bullet had even touched him.

Clint was impressed with the other man's speed. It had seemed to come out of nowhere, which meant that all of Teaghan's men probably had similar skills hidden away like aces tucked up their sleeves. But Clint wasn't one to be taken by surprise very often and he shifted his own tactics as well.

Remembering how a boxer outguesses his opponent, Clint watched the other man's body instead of his face or eyes. Disregarding everything else, Clint spotted a slight shifting of the man's weight from one foot to the other.

The man with the goatee snapped his head the opposite way as though he was going to charge in that direction. Clint saw that as well and damn near reacted to it, but forced himself to focus on what the man's body was doing rather than what his face was saying.

After all, no matter what he meant to do, the man with the goatee had to shift his weight to do it. His eyes darted to the right and even his hands moved that way, but Clint ignored both of those things and aimed the Colt at a spot that was off to the other man's left.

Clint fired at the same time that the other man made his true move. Goatee might have seen that Clint hadn't taken the bait, but it was too late to change his direction. His body was already committed to his move and his momentum carried him straight into the spot where Clint had been aiming.

The Colt barked once more and the other man was there to catch the bullet. Hot lead drilled through his chest and he kept right on moving until his face hit the dirt. After a few twitches, his body was still and this time, it would stay that way.

"Warren!" Teaghan yelled at the man who was still shifting groggily upon the ground. "Get your ass up! Pete! Where the hell are you?"

Teaghan had been standing partially in the doorway, looking crazily in all directions. When his eyes stopped and focused on one spot, it was like a written sign, which Clint had no trouble reading.

As he turned to face that same direction, Clint dropped straight down, listening to a sudden tense feeling in his gut. Even before he felt his body's impact with the ground, Clint heard a gunshot echo through the air and something whip by his head like an angry hornet.

Still unable to see exactly where the shooter was, Clint started rolling away from Teaghan's building while bringing his Colt up to eye level. Another shot came, this time punching a hole in the dirt less than an inch from Clint's face. The impact kicked up enough grit to sting his eyes, but not before Clint had gotten a glimpse at where the big man with the full beard was standing.

Part of Clint's mind was wondering how the big man had run down from where he'd been looking out a window and gotten to the street without making a sound. The rest of his mind was focusing on that brief glimpse he had gotten before his vision was smeared by dirt that brought water to his eyes.

Clint pointed the Colt as if he were aiming at a painting in his mind's eye. He pulled his trigger three times, covering a spread of space in the picture still lingering where the other man had been standing. When he jumped to his feet and cleared his eyes, Clint saw the bearded man standing right in front of him, staring him right in the eyes.

Pete started to lift his gun and a snarl moved across his face. Just then, not one, but two spots on his dark suit turned an even darker shade. Pete's eyes dropped and so did his gun arm as more and more blood seeped out through the fresh holes in his chest and stomach.

As much as he wanted to fire his gun, Pete simply didn't have the strength. He didn't even have the strength to stay standing and crumpled down onto his knees before falling over dead.

Teaghan stepped out from where he'd been hiding and stood in front of his unmarked storefront. His eyes went

calmly from one prone body in the dirt to another, coming
to a rest upon Clint.

Clint flipped open the Colt's cylinder and dumped out
the spent casings. He took quick stock of the situation and
saw that Warren was still down and somewhat out of it,
but the taller man who'd been following him was nowhere
to be found.

"This is pointless, Mr. Adams," Teaghan said. He'd
already drawn his gun, but seemed hesitant to point it
even though Clint was still in the process of reloading.
There was no fear in his eyes; merely caution and pa-
tience. "I or my remaining men can gun you down at will.
What more do you plan on doing here?"

"Me?" Clint responded. "I don't plan on doing much
more. They, on the other hand . . ." He paused and turned
his eyes upward as several dozen shutters and doors in
neighboring buildings swung open to reveal the faces of
several dozen locals. Each of those faces was peering out
from behind a rifle, pistol or shotgun.

Looking back to Teaghan, Clint finished his statement.
"They intend on taking their town back."

FORTY-THREE

"What the hell is this?" Teaghan snarled as he spun and looked at all the faces staring back at him.

Clint nodded and fit the last round into the cylinder of his Colt. "A friend of mine and I had a talk with most everyone in town. You see, that's how I spent the time you so graciously gave me. I told them I meant to show up here and have a talk with you and that if they wanted to join me, they were more than welcome."

Teaghan laughed at Clint and all the faces around him, but it sounded forced and not at all as comfortable as his normal tone of voice. "You think these shopkeepers can back me down? Hell, I even see some women up in those windows. I'll bet they're having a hard time keeping their guns pointed in the right direction."

"Maybe," Clint said. "Maybe not. But I'll bet once they all start pulling their triggers, a few of them will find their mark once this whole street fills with flying lead."

"So this is your big plan, Mr. Adams?"

"Yeah. Actually, I'd say it's a pretty good one. Why not ask the James gang, or the Younger brothers, or the Daltons? They've had run-ins with plenty of straight-shooters, but once a whole town gets together and sets its mind to something, they can tear down the toughest gangs out there. Jesse and Frank were damn lucky to make it out alive from a situation very much like this. A whole lot of their gang wasn't so lucky."

Clint had been saying those things for the benefit of all the nervous locals as well as to rattle Teaghan. Judging by the looks on all the faces he could see, Clint figured he'd succeeded on both counts.

"So what do you say, Teaghan?" Clint asked. "You ready to clean up your mess and leave town?"

After thinking it over for a moment, Teaghan glanced in another direction and said one word.

"Dave."

Clint had lost sight of the tall gunman for some time. The moment he heard Teaghan call out the killer's name, he knew he had only a second or so before Dave would step out from where he'd been hiding and take his shot. From everything he'd heard when talking to the locals about Teaghan's men, Dave sounded like he'd done all his killings up-close. That meant he would probably do the same thing now, rather than pick Clint off from a distance using a rifle.

Of course, there was always a first time for everything.

Figuring he had about fifty-fifty odds, Clint closed his eyes and waited for the one thing he could rely on at that moment and time.

Coming from the direction where Teaghan had been looking, Clint heard a sound that he immediately recognized. It was the same sound he'd heard only minutes ago when he'd made his walk down Mesa Street and Military Avenue.

The crunch could have come from any set of boots, but Clint had been listening so closely before that he would have been able to remember that sound in the middle of a busy street at the start of a business day.

He snapped the Colt's cylinder shut with the flick of his wrist and swiveled on the balls of his feet toward that distinctive footfall. Giving himself a split second to make sure he wasn't about to shoot an innocent passerby, Clint got a glimpse of Dave's face and fired from the hip.

The Colt and Dave's gun went off simultaneously. Dave, however, had been caught in mid-stride a fraction of a second before he could aim. Dave's round hissed through the air and took a chunk of meat from Clint's forearm, but Clint's bullet punched a clean hole through Dave's forehead.

The tall killer was dead before he flopped down into the dirt.

"Warren."

That single word hit Clint harder than the lead that had just burned through his flesh. He knew Warren was directly behind him. Clint also knew he wouldn't be able to turn, aim and fire before Warren got a chance to take a few shots of his own. And with Warren being so close, there was little chance that he would miss.

Teaghan's single command didn't even have enough time to echo from the walls before the air was filled with the crackle of multiple gunshots. The thunder came from all around Clint and even from over his head.

Lead whipped through the air as smoke billowed from no fewer than eight or nine nearby windows. All of that gunfire converged on one general area and Warren started to dance like a fish that had been tossed onto dry land as a bullet found its way into his body.

From what Clint could see by the time he turned around, more of the locals' shots had missed than hit, but the job was still very much done. Warren's hand was outstretched, still ready to put a round into Clint's back. The rest of him, however, was a bloody mess and he spat out his last breath before falling face-first.

Clint looked up gratefully and saw that every local he'd talked to was there. Even Sandra Rigsby was among the nervous faces who'd shown up to lend their support and rise up against the man who'd kept them all under his thumb.

"So what do you say now?" asked one of several local men who'd stepped out to hold Teaghan at gunpoint. "Any more lessons you want to teach us?"

Teaghan didn't say a word, even though it looked as if it were tearing him apart to remain silent. Instead, he tossed his gun down and shook his head.

"Come on then," the local said, nudging Teaghan with the barrel of his shotgun. "You've got some cleaning up to do."

The rest of the night was spent as one giant celebration. Groups of locals took turns supervising Teaghan as the former town boss was made to sift through the ashes of the sheriff's office and find the bodies of the men who'd died there. The next day, Teaghan was to dig their graves and bury them properly.

Clint stood at the bar of Paco's Cantina and tipped back one of several free beers.

"That was one hell of a show," said a man who'd stepped up to stand beside Clint.

Clint didn't have to look over to know the man was Brandon Morris. "Yes. It sure was."

"So what's next? For me, I mean?"

"That was something else I discussed with everyone else in town," Clint said. "As far as I or anyone else could see, you may have gone about things wrong, but you sure as hell weren't in Teaghan's league. You're a business-man. I'd say a damn good one since you own almost all the saloons in town."

"Nah. Just The Rusty Spur."

Clint shook his head and smiled. "I've only seen a few other places kept in such good shape as The Spur and they're all here. That's either a big coincidence or shared management, and I'm not a big believer of coincidence."

"All right. So I own a good part of this town. As soon as you leave, these people may still string me up no matter what I own."

"Yeah. They just might. You could either round up your men and leave or start using your business sense properly. It seems like you're a better saloon owner than an outlaw anyway. The money's better too, I'd bet."

Brandon stepped back and looked at Clint as though he couldn't believe what he was seeing. More importantly, he looked as though he couldn't believe what he was hearing. There were plenty of older men watching Brandon carefully, so Brandon picked one of those and went over to talk. The locals were more than ready to listen.

Clint finished his beer and headed out. The locals didn't need him there any longer. Cielo Grande didn't need him.

The balance had been tipped and it would stay in their favor.

Clint walked away with a satisfied grin. There was a blonde that he didn't want to keep waiting any longer.

She needed him.

Watch for

THE HANGING TREE

269th novel in the exciting GUNSMITH series
from Jove

Coming in May!

J. R. ROBERTS

THE GUNSMITH